Quinn Checks In

IAN LOOME

(writing as 'LH Thomson')

DEDICATION

For my father John, a great man.

CONTENTS

ACKNOWLEDGMENTS

All characters in this novel are fictitious. I'd like to thank the many Philadelphians who offered advice on locations, accents and more, writers RP Dahlke and Joe Konrath for the advice and the readers on Goodreads who encouraged me

1.

IN ART, THE ARC OF A CURVE can be a beautiful and important thing. In Art Deco, for example, the consistency of its curves gives each design a sense of cleanliness and function, of uniformity.

When I was an art forger, a perfect curve was one of my best friends.

So believe me when I say that the arc of the pool cue slicing through the air towards my head was a thing of beauty, a mighty cut that, in that split second, with Boston's classic rocker '*Smoking*' cranking on the jukebox in the corner, made me wonder why the giant biker swinging it had opted for a life of vice and violence, instead of baseball.

My name is Liam Quinn, and I've been a fighter most of my life. One of the blessings of a decade of boxing is a sort of athletic 'sixth sense'. Some pros call it being "in the zone", that split second when your adrenaline peaks, your instincts take over, and everything just seems to slow…

Right.

Down.

I ducked, dropping between the two tree-trunk arms around my chest, and the pool cue continued its arc. If he'd swung with a tighter reach, instead of stepping into it so directly, he'd have come up short and gone over my head while still missing his enormous bald-and-goateed companion.

But then it wouldn't have been perfect.

Instead, the cue smashed into his buddy's temple with a hollow clack, like a brick dropped on hard cement.

The big one behind me went down in a pile of sleeveless denim and biker boots. The cue stick splintered, the thicker handle rattling on the old hardwood floor. The immediate shock of the mistake froze his friend in front of me for a moment, a look of surprise under his greasy red Viking hair and poor facial grooming.

I was already crouched, so it made sense to throw the uppercut. It's never been my strongest punch – I'm more a stick-and-move guy, despite being close to a heavyweight, so I favor my hook. But I had a substantial tactical advantage, and I came up hard, nailing him with my right hand pretty much flush on the button, that helpful cluster of nerves at the end of the chin.

His knees buckled, his eyes rolled back, and he crumpled like a pup tent in heavy wind, the pool cue clattering to the ground and rolling away.

It hadn't taken more than about fifteen seconds for the whole fight, including the time to tap the cue swinger on the shoulder. But everyone in the dingy pool hall had stopped to stare, and the only sound was the blaring tune. Cigarettes hung from hairy lips. Beers were held aloft, untipped. Light streamed into the room from the wall of filthy windows overlooking the strip mall's parking lot, cutting through grime, the haze of illegal smoke and the frozen action on row after row of green-felt tables.

It was the kind of place where you could smell the urinals ten feet before the bathroom door and half the customers even sooner. I wondered how many of less-than-reputable locals knew the bikers.

But it didn't seem too likely; neither was supposed to be in North Philly. The big guy swinging the cue was Abel Larsson. He and his bear-hugging buddy were Devil Deacons, bikers from South Philly, and they were avoiding their home turf because Abel was legally dead … at least according to the State of Pennsylvania.

Smokin', smokin'

We're cookin' tonight,
  just keep on tokin'

The jukebox kept blaring the tune, pool balls slowing to a halt, no one moving to line up the next shot.

My employer – the Philadelphia Mutual Insurance Co. – was not convinced, and before paying out to the charmingly gold-toothed Mrs. Larsson, my boss had sent me to check into it. I'd started at the trailer park where most of them hung out. The good citizens had informed me that Abel was persona non grata before his passing. First, they'd told me to practise walking in heavy traffic. Then they'd directed me to an old loner at the last trailer to the right, a crusty old biker with a false left leg and a body odour designed to kill vampires.

He'd sat on his porch whittling a stick into something suspiciously shiv like, while I'd explained why his claim was suspicious.

"Uh huh," he'd offered, before horking up a throatful of phlegm and depositing it ten feet in front of him with a mighty spit. "If he wasn't freakin' dead, he'd be freakin' dead for makin' us think he was freakin' dead," was the way he'd put it. "Now, you find out he's not dead, you come back here and tell us. We'll make sure of it for you."

Of course, Larsson's less-than-professional death certificate couldn't have fooled Stevie Wonder after a three-day-bender. It looked like someone had used Microsoft Paint.

"Hey!" The pockmarked, ratty-looking guy in the leather vest behind the pockmarked, ratty-looking bar was pissed.

"What?"

"This ain't that kind of place. No fights! I got a license to worry about."

I looked around at the collected decades of jailhouse experience: big, small, hairy, skinhead. The dozen customers would've made any child educator question the validity of their profession. They were covered in almost as many scars as tats, and more denim and leather than a cow in a Levis factory.

"Seriously? That's your objection?"

There was a low murmur of laughter around the room and most people went back to their games. Someone cracked a set of pool balls a dozen feet away.

A fat guy sitting at the end of the bar interrupted, getting the barman's attention. He had grease stains on his grey sweatshirt. Sweat stains, too. His eyes were dark and droopy, his beard more an unkept, wispy mess than the real thing. "Hey Walt, how come youse almonds taste like bacon?"

"What? Shuddup, will ya!? I'm talking to this guy."

"Yeah... well, I'm just saying."

"Saying what?"

"That almonds shouldn't taste like bacon. That's just weird, man. I mean... did you have bacon bits in the bowl before and not wash it?"

"Jesus tapdancing..."

"And if that's it, then what does that say about the hygiene here?"

The barman shook his head. "They're *smoked*, ya idjit." Then he turned back to me.

I said, "So, on the available evidence..."

"Yeah, well, maybe it is that kind of joint. But take it outside. I already get enough of that crap and I got a license to worry about."

"I didn't start the fight," I reminded him. I had tried to be polite about it. To an extent. Abel had said something nasty about my mother, which is a no go, because my mother is a freakin' saint. I'd reminded him that his mother wouldn't find that very polite, and would most certainly tell him herself, if she ever got her face out of my crotch.

6

From there, the discourse had progressed in a southerly direction.

"I don't care who started it, or who finished it. I care that I've got a broken pool cue, broken glass to cleanup and a pair of unconscious morons staining the hardwood. Plus, it sends a bad message to the rest of the patrons..."

"Smoked?" the fat bar patron asked. "Like, smoked with bacon? Like the peanuts were wrapped in bacon...?"

"... Who ain't exactly what you'd call 'gifted' to begin with in the judgment and poor impulse control department. You get my drift?" He turned back to the regular. "Hickory smoked, ya moron! Like bacon is cured with hickory smoke? They use it on the peanuts. Jesus Tapdancing Murphy..."

I looked down at the two prone men. "I do. I do get your drift, there, Walt, and I feel real bad. You want to help carry them out?"

"Very funny."

"I try."

He plopped a sawed-off shotgun onto the bar. "Still funny?"

"Not so much."

"Smart. You're not from this neck of the woods. I'd remember anyone this annoying."

"Fishtown. You know the Druid up on..."

"Yeah, I know it. Marty DiSilvio's place. We used to beat their ass in slo pitch back in the day. All them ex-cops, they sure couldn't handle their beer and slo-pitch at the same time." Walt put his hands on his hips, imperious about victories past. "Somebody owes me fifteen-fifty for the pool, thirty-seven dollars for the pool cue, and twelve bucks for the pitcher of beer."

I pulled out my smartphone and took pictures of the two prone men as they snoozed by the pool table then went over to the bar and threw down four twenties. "Keep the change and sorry for the trouble."

"You stay that generous, you can come back and punch out guys whenever. I mean… try not to leave them where I've got to clean stuff up, but…"

"I'll keep it in mind," I said.

"And if they or the other Deacons inquire as to who it was whipped their asses?"

"Eh… tell them to call Philly Mutual, ask for Ramon."

"Huh…"

"What?"

The regular answered on his behalf. "You don't look much like a Ramon. Too pasty."

"I'm not. Ramon's the guy who signs the checks. I'm Liam. Liam Quinn."

The bartender nodded, then frowned as if remembering something. "Hey… wait a second: I remember that name. Didn't you used to fight middleweight…"

"Light heavy. But just Silver Gloves, a year of Golden…"

"Yeah! Yeah, that's right. There was some big talk about you on the amateur fight scene."

"I guess."

"So… what the Hell happened!?"

I shrugged. "You know how it is…"

"Yeah… I guess."

Ouch. But he wasn't wrong.

I headed down the stairs – with a couple of glances back over my shoulder, for safety's sake – and out the front door, into the afternoon sun and the crowded little parking lot.

2.

I didn't mind picking up the tab for the pool cue.

As a freelance insurance investigator, I'd get a two-and-a-half percent recovery fee, and Larsson's policy had been worth a hundred grand. That was a twenty-five-hundred-dollar payday, my best single paycheck in a year on the job.

My boss, the ever-serious Ramon Garcia de Soria, would be as close as he got to happy. Every time I saved the company money, it made it a little easier for him to justify his little experiment in hiring me to the rest of middle management.

My gold '81 Firebird – an unfinished project of my father's, complete with original motor and equally original rust primer patches – was next to a couple of Harleys. I momentarily pondered kicking them over. It was juvenile, and I'm not proud. But it would've been funny anyway, as they were so parked so close, they'd have gone over like dominos.

I couldn't be sure, however, that they belonged to my two guys; and besides, they had enough problems ahead of them: aside from the fraud charges and the inevitable civil suit from PMI, they'd have to explain to the Devil Deacons why they'd skipped out on their brethren.

You hang around bad people, bad things happen. This is something I've learned from way too much personal experience.

I got in and fired up the big motor, listening to it rattle like a shelf full of milk jugs.

The sun cut warmly through the windshield. One day, the bearings were going to give out and the whole damn block was going to drop out the bottom, and I could finally tell my father her day was done. But on this occasion, after a few more frightening rattles and me holding the ignition key in the start position for a few seconds, it roared into … Ok, "roared" is generous … it kicked to life.

I grabbed my aviators from under the radio and slipped them on to cut the glare, before pulling the car out onto the quiet city street, shocks giving a little too much as she rode over the ridge of asphalt at the exit.

I love driving through the city in the day, feeling the energy of it, the vibrancy. Plus, concentrating on traffic takes my mind off other garbage.

As I said earlier, I used to be a forger. My love of art and creativity had taken me down a strange road. I never figured I had the talent to make it myself in the art world – or the patience to work with people in the art community, who can be as emotionally fragile and unstable as any creative type.

But I'd spent years learning to paint and draw in a variety of styles, and when you get out of college, you need to make a buck more than just about anything. My father, a tough, old-school policeman, had helped pay for my education, through the nose. I felt almost obliged to make something of my training, pay the old man back somehow.

Forgery wouldn't have been his first choice... but it wouldn't have been mine, either.

I'm not going to lie: I was great at it.

It had started innocently enough, selling a few reproductions of famous paintings, honest about the fact that they weren't the real thing. The crime part – hanging out with criminals, working for criminals, selling forgeries to the pretentious and distracted – was where things went south.

It's funny how you get caught up: one day you're worrying about paying bills, about whether you'll be able to keep that first apartment or need to move back in with Ma and Pa.

The next, some guy is telling you how much talent you

have and slipping you an envelope with ten grand in it. You're hanging around rich folks, going to big parties where you recognize people even though you don't know them, making a name in the world as a "legitimate art dealer", wearing nice suits and dating pretty, vacuous sleeve holders.

And then it all comes crashing down. The illusion shatters, reputations in tatters, and you have to start thinking about the real price.

I'd gotten pinched at age twenty-seven, while running a "gallery" as a front for moving copies of Asian masters. Then I'd done three-and-a-half years in the pen – Curran-Fromhold Correctional Facility -- much to the embarrassment of my family and everyone in the old neighborhood.

Ah, hell… I deserved it. They knew it, I knew it, and everybody knew it.

When I was released, a condition of my parole was that I wasn't allowed to pick up a brush until I'd been out for a year and found a suitably less-tempting occupation. Ramon, whose brother had done time and had worked in a prison placement program, took pity on my lousy job prospects. He figured an ex-boxer with an art history degree, some experience grifting and two cops in his immediate family would have a good nose for other frauds.

He'd pulled a bunch of strings to get me a provisional private investigator's license, so I owed him. And by keeping me as a freelancer – a condition of my remaining on the straight-and-narrow – he didn't have to pay me a salary, just the commission. He liked that I worked cheap.

There was only so much art fraud or theft to investigate, of course, and I'd had to adapt to the likes of Larsson and company. In the months since I'd been out, I'd gotten accustomed to the fact that, no matter how in the wrong they were, no one on the face of God's green Earth likes their insurance company.

Traffic was light on the northwest side of town, and I turned on 97.5, The Fanatic, to get a score in the Phillies game, an early start against Florida. They were arguing about whether pro athletes earn their ridiculous contracts, with the debate focussing on owners making even more. In Philadelphia, pro sports are right up there with God and country on peoples' priority lists. Recent years notwithstanding – Go Birds – being a Philly fan can be painful. Living in Philly, with its crime, endless traffic delays and political graft so rampant they might as well have issued their own currency gives people license to bitch.

Combine the two and you get… sports radio at its finest. The inevitable point about teams cooking the books to show losses ensued, and after five minutes, no one had bothered to suggest maybe the profits or revenue base were too high, and season ticket holders were the ones being hosed. I wasn't any closer to knowing how the boys had done, so I switched over to the news talk station and let the voices drift into the background as I maneuvered through the congestion.

As grimy as that pool hall had been, most of the cases I handled weren't even that interesting – staking out a compensation cheat, or getting video of a so-called whiplash victim who could still swing a golf club, maybe checking into some HMO double-billing.

But when a forgery or art theft came up, they had the right guy on staff.

I drove quickly and nimbly, patient with slowdowns after years of dealing with Philly's one-way streets and endless construction seasons. I like the narrow thoroughfares here, the city's odd mix of centuries of history blending with a modern glass-and-steel feel.

The pay for the Larsson case was good, but the work wasn't exactly what you'd call fulfilling. Abel had left a trail so obvious it might as well have been sprayed in fluorescent paint; and, like most goons, his idea of laying low until he got his settlement didn't extend to the common sense of getting out of town for a while, or even not spending money he hadn't yet been given, which is why he was risking a roll on the green felt. He was no Einstein.

There were plenty of spots in the parking lot of the company's downtown offices and I pulled in between a green Volkswagen and a Honda street bike. The investigative division was on an anonymous floor of a twenty-three-story tinted glass building. Past the front door was a reception desk. The receptionist, Angela, ignored me as usual. Beyond her the room was divided into a series of cubicles.

Ramon was standing by Mike McPhee's, the first in the row, trying to convince Mike to add a case to his backlog. He was gesticulating, making some effusive point, selling the case's benefits.

The firm's ten investigators all had files of five or six investigations at any one time, as PMI is one of the largest insurers in the state. But at fifty-three, Mike was the office veteran, an overweight, jowly ex-cop with a silver-grey crew-cut. His backlog was particularly heavy, perhaps twice the norm, and in the world of the supposedly paperless office, his Formica cubicle was generally covered in the stuff, the piles obscuring the notes and pictures he'd pinned to its back wall

Ramon looked tired, leaning one arm on Mike's desk, his pale yellow knit tie pulled down and his collar undone, sleeves rolled up, grey suit vest hanging open, no jacket.

"Come on, Mike. This is right up your alley. Head down to the stadium, ask a few questions, catch a bit of the game at the team's expense. You love soccer, right?"

"I love the New York Red Bulls. The Red Bulls. Not the Union. Worst part about living in this damn city, having to see that team win games.

"You might get season tickets out of it."

"So? For the privilege of rooting for someone else's home team, I get to do a stakeout with the Sons of Ben? Forget it. I'd rather have a root canal. Send junior there." He gestured vaguely in my direction.

I kind of hoped Ramon would take him up on it. The Union's fan club were one heck of a party, before and after kickoff.

No such luck.

"I got an art case for Quinn. Besides, you should be honored to watch a real club play instead of those over-hyped fools from Jersey."

"So... he gets the money case, I get the shaft? Where does the part where I'm the senior guy and actually on staff come into play?"

"Mikey, it's just a booze theft, a dozen missing kegs of cheap draft from the stadium. Chances are you look at the security tape, you figure there's no way to ID the guys who broke in, we write it off." He was talking with his hands, which usually meant he wanted the conversation to wrap up. "So, go to a few games, see if you can shake something loose. Speaking of which..." He turned to me. "What you got, kid? That tip on Abel Larsson work out?"

I filled him in and showed him the pictures. He slapped me on the back, "Good job, Quinn, good job. I mean... don't knock the idiots out if you don't have to, but other than that..."

Then he shot a look of irritation at Mike and at Paul Forman, a thin, bespectacled guy who'd just entered from the corridor at the other end of the room.

Forman, who legend had it could be pushed over by a stiff breeze, had a file folder in one hand and a coffee in the other, and held both up as he shrugged. "What? What'd I do?"

Ramon shook his head. "Never mind. But you could

both learn a little about work ethic from the jailbird."

Like my dad, Ramon was another ex-cop, so he was still wary that I'd return to the dark side and do something stupid. I think that he figured reminding everyone would force me to prove him wrong. He's that kind of guy,a always concerned with the example he sets.

He shouldn't have worried. I figured some things out while inside, important things about not ignoring that angel on your shoulder, and not trying to take the easy way. When I was a fighter, I was a stick-and-move guy, so I should've learned to rack up the points. Instead, I went for the knockout and it sometimes cost me big time.

But learning from that was nothing like the patience you learn doing hard time.

True, my forgery victims had been the kind of rich people who deserved to be in jail themselves, not the philanthropic, charitable types. Mist of my take had gone to help other people, because I come from a tough neighborhood, where people need a hand. But wrong was wrong, and karma had taught me a hard lesson about taking the easy way out.

And I wasn't Robin Hood. I robbed from the rich and gave to myself, as well.

I said, "What's the case?"

Ramon walked towards his small corner office and motioned for me to follow. Once we were both inside, he closed the door. "This one's kind of personal."

I got the implication: that I didn't need the others in the office knowing I was doing the boss a favor. But I did need the case – I was still paying back my court-ordered restitution, with a quarter-million dollars to go.

Don't ever let anyone suggest to you that penalties aren't deterrents. That was one big bill to have to pay, believe me.

He handed me a photo of a young woman. She was tall

and beautiful: dark almond eyes, tanned skin, her wavy brown hair streaked with color. "Alison Pace. She's the manager of a small gallery on Chestnut, the DeGoey. She's also a friend of Nora's from college."

I looked down at the small photo of his daughter on his desk. She had dark red hair, from her Irish mother's side, and olive skin from Ramon. I'd known Nora since we were kids. She'd gone on to great success and was now an associate curator at the Philadelphia Museum of Art – that's the big building behind the statue of Rocky Balboa, by the way, although it could be a fireworks display if Nora was nearby, and I still wouldn't see it.

She'd always had that effect on me; that voodoo that caught my gaze and held it suspended, elevated, like a kite in an updraft. Nora was pure class: smart, beautiful, refined and graceful, a tall drink of water with high cheekbones and a higher IQ. The idea of her liking a guy like me – slightly crooked nose from boxing, the little scars on my chin and my eyebrow, and the obvious-but-less-visible scars on the inside – seemed about as remote as a career as a painter.

And once that career went south, any chances of us went with it.

But… that was okay. I was never in her league anyhow, not really. Oh sure, you keep your hair neat, dress nice, flash the baby blues at some women. I did okay. But Nora was no average woman. She was grace and poise; she was the smooth arc of a perfect curve.

So naturally, I'd never even asked her on a date, and probably never would. We were just friends. Good friends, at that. She had a secret yearning, I think, to follow in her father's footsteps as a cop. So we'd work on the odd insurance case together. She was a great resource, both on local artists and on the business. And if we were both honest, we just liked sitting around shooting the bull.

Ramon continued. "Pair of heavies hit Pace's gallery yesterday, during a limited showing of a painting by the Dutch master Johannes Vermeer."

"Heavy hitter. Big name for a small gallery. Anything new from him on the market would be in the tens of millions."

"There were a few other artists in the show. They fleshed it out with some theme, a bunch of local talents."

"Vermeer's specialty was impressionist interiors, although he had some fine portraits, as well. The other workers were probably something on those lines. But he was a real master, so they won't have held the same allure."

He looked at me quickly sideways. I got the sense art interested him abut as much as TV infomercials. "Yeah... whatever. Anyway, two guys, dark bomber jackets, stockings over their heads, blue jeans, black boots, shotguns."

"Professionals?"

"Such as they are."

"They took the Vermeer?"

"And only."

"Gallery had security?"

"Couple of old guys, rent-a-cops. They hit the floor like they had rocks in their pockets. Nobody was blaming them, mind. They get paid jack diddly."

"Who was the lead?" The 'lead' is the principle investigating officer, usually a detective.

"Bill Trevanian."

"Ah... Hell."

Bill Trevanian was old-school, a fifty-something detective who'd been a SWAT guy after serving in Iraq, then worked Homicide for a decade before moving to vice, then robbery. He had a ginger flat-top crewcut and a pack-a-day Marlboro habit. He was legendary for taking down some hard-time scumbags, armed robbers of Pat Delaney's ilk chief among them.

He also hated me on a deeply personal level. His nogoodnik cousin, Shawn, bought one of my forgeries – knowing full well, mind you, that it was a forgery – then got pinched in their ensuing investigation into my world.

"They weren't expecting any problems, obviously," Ramon said.

"Seems naïve, keeping something that valuable without significant protection. The thieves didn't grab anything else, not even stuff near the door?"

"No. And the gallery had never had any problems that I know of. The Vermeer had already been on display for most of the week."

"Their guard was down. Makes sense. What's the exposure?"

"They're covered for up to ten million in theft, so the Vermeer would be full-value. That's a big hit for the company unless we can recover. You're going to be able to handle this?"

It meant my cut could be huge if I recovered the painting and proved it was stolen, two-point-five percent. Normally, that doesn't amount to much. In this case, it was a quarter-million dollars. It would pay off my outstanding fines.

It wasn't the kind of opportunity I could afford to turn down; even if I could, I hated to think how Nora or my parents would react. Any suggestion I wasn't going all-out in my efforts to go straight would terrify the Hell out of them.

"Twist my rubber arm, boss," I said, heading out of his office. "And hey, throw in that missing booze case at the same time."

Mikey looked over, both hands clasped together in front of himself as if praising my name.

"Quinn, you magnificent bastard! Thank you, thank you, thank you for not subjecting me to that piece of garbage soccer club of yours."

For free Union tickets, I could live with the insult. I loved it down at the park, just across the Barry Bridge from Jersey. Besides, the way the Union had been playing, I'd get the last word.

And now Mike owed me a favor.

3.

The gallery was downtown on Chestnut, an intermittently trendy one-way shopping street that was increasingly having a tough time holding down tenants, more a victim of the national economic scene than anything.

It wasn't that the landlords weren't trying. People just weren't willing to be adventurous with their capital. Consequently, the street's identity was pockmarked, shell-shocked. For every neat little gallery or dance studio there was a franchise restaurant or copy shop taking advantage of the cheap rent.

The gallery was in an old red-brick building, across from a Five Guys Burger and Fries, a point of reference I bring up for no reason other than liking their burgers. The sign was in silver, but was understated, with a blend of two squared-off sans serif fonts: "DeGoey Fine Art."

Inside, the floors were honey maple and the walls were whitewashed, cast in bright lights from a variety of spotlights and fixtures; a variety of paintings graced the walls: impressionist, modern, pop art, some surreal cubist work, some nuts-and-bolts realism; some large, some small, most framed tastefully. A handful of small sculptures helped divide the room with abstract poise.

A few years earlier, I could have spent hours there, just studying the heart and brilliance, all in such a confined area. The angry streaks of rich ochre and purple, the natural greens and yellows from nature, pleading for calm.

When I was a little kid, my parents thought my art fascination was cute; they'd take me to the museum and show me off, have me identify each painting's artist without looking, then have me announce the answers loudly to the surprise of people passing by. Until I hit my teens and started boxing, I think even my old man kind of enjoyed that.

A greeting board by the entrance desk confirmed my earlier guess: "Interiors. A retrospective across four hundred years," it read. I picked up the brochure that sat on the nearby table. Most of the artists showing were modern, but along with the Vermeer there had been a handful of standard bearers from the seventeenth- and eighteenth-century English school: Cranch, Thomas Phillips, and a lesser-regarded Beechey.

There was no sign of any police presence, which meant the forensic team had either been quick and thorough or quick and sloppy. Hopefully the former; for all the heat they take in the papers, the boys in blue usually had the right intentions. And most of the detectives I'd ever met were just wizards at figuring out puzzles.

By the end of the day, they'd probably know what shoes the guys who hit the place were wearing; people would be surprised to know how much information they can get off a security tape once they've had it enhanced and studied by a keen-eyed investigator.

"May I help you?"

"I certainly hope so."

The question came from a short blonde woman in a grey flannel skirt and red-striped white shirt. It worked about as poorly as that sounds, although the horned-rim glasses were a nice touch. She looked like a secretary who'd swallowed a candy striper.

She smiled back and looked down at her shoes for a quick second. "We're having sort of a couple of tough days, actually."

"I heard." I took out my pocket notepad.

"Ah. Look, I can't talk to the press..."

"Not a reporter. I'm looking for Alison Pace. I'm with

21

Philadelphia Mutual."

She scanned me from top to bottom then frowned, raising one quizzical eyebrow. "You don't look like an insurance guy."

"I'm not. I'm a freelance investigator. The company likes to check out any potentially large claim as early as it can after an incident, to make sure we get the facts as consistent as possible."

I'd used the line enough times in the last year to make it second-nature, like ordering a favorite pizza.

"Oh. Okay, Mr…"

"It's Liam," I said, offering a hand. "Liam Quinn. Ms…?"

She shook my hand quickly and held it there for a moment. "Oh. Stephanie. Stephanie Smith."

I smiled at her again but said nothing. After a moment, she realized she was staring at me without speaking and released my hand.

She said, "Why do I feel like I should be saying or doing something right now?"

Women are strange sometimes. I mean, she just sort of froze, like her software needed rebooting or something. Maybe she recognized me from somewhere.

I said, "Alison Pace? You were going to find her…?"

She pulled her papers close to her chest for a moment. "Yes! Exactly, yes. Just…wait here for a moment, Mr. Liam…. Quinn. Mr. Quinn."

Like I said, strange.

She came back with Pace a few moments later. Alison's picture hadn't done her justice; she was stunning, the face of a model in a cream business suit, offset with small and tasteful gold jewelry accents. She offered a hand and shook perfunctorily. No wedding ring, I noticed.

"I hope this isn't going to take too long, Mr. Quinn. I

understand Nora's father wants to help…"

"It's not just that," I said. "We're a coverage holder on your theft policy. Of the police can't figure this out, we're out a whole bunch of money and your premiums go up. A lot of the time, if there aren't solid leads in the first forty-eight hours, a case can go south."

"Mainly, the takeaway is that our premiums go up," she deadpanned. "That painting was one of the oldest of the fully established Vermeers. Do you know what that could go for at auction?"

"I'm guessing seven figures."

"Try eight."

"Ouch." I did some mental math, trying to picture that many zeroes after a one. It made my head hurt, so I gave up.

"Of course, I don't suppose they could sell it for ten million or more stolen, Mr. Quinn. But they had plenty of motives. Therefore, the insurance hit on this would be huge for both of us."

"Mainly."

"Well, like I said, I don't know what I can add that wasn't in the police report. They sat down with me for more than an hour." She looked weary of the entire thing.

"Yeah … but there's not much chance I'm going to see that this decade."

"I don't understand."

"Well, the police don't have to share their report with the victim or the victim's insurance company. And I have some history with them that doesn't improve the odds. Plus, they don't like sharing what they have in general. It's a real closed shop, the police department."

She thought about it for a moment. "I have a list of the people there on the day whom the police interviewed, including the two guards; but frankly, I'm not sure what good it's going to do you: as soon as they came in with the

23

shotguns and told everybody to get down, we were all flat on our faces in a moment. Nobody was real brave or anything."

"Understandable. Someone waved a shotgun at me, I'd get down, too."

She studied me again. "Really?"

I smiled. "I can handle myself in a pinch, but there's a certain lack of respect for physics and biology when you ignore the power of a firearm."

"You make it sound less cowardly than it felt, if I'm being honest. When it happened..." She crossed her arms defensively. "Well... it's hard to explain."

"No one is going to knock your for being terrified of dying," I suggested. "People who aren't scared when a gun is drawn on them probably have a few screws loose."

She smiled faintly. "Thank you. That helps."

"Our motto: making you feel less lousy about your losses."

She frowned. "Really?"

"No. Joke."

"Ah."

The look said my timing was poor, which was nothing new. The joke, too. Also nothing new. I've been told I'm funny... but it's nearly always by some guy who isn't, some dude with a career criminal record and the lightheartedness of a lump of lead.

I got back to the point. "So... they came in, fired that shot..." I pointed at the damage to the plaster above, "... then got everyone down on the ground?"

"Yeah," she said. Her gaze was a little distant, and she was obviously upset at the memory. "The smaller guy told everyone to keep their eyes ahead. He said, 'If anyone looks up, I'll blow their heads off.'"

"Scary. Plus, terrifying grammar. I mean, it's Philly, so no one's keeping score of plurals and singular possessives, but..."

She stared at me blankly.

"Do go on," I offered.

"One guy was short, one tall. The short one seemed to be in charge because he told the other guy to hurry up."

"And the other guy?"

"Tall, stocky. He had a tummy. He didn't say anything, that I recall."

"So, the big guy, he went to the front?"

"No, the back. The short one went to the front of the room, where the Vermeer was."

"The other guy was... what, just keeping guard from behind the people on the ground?

"I couldn't see him, but he was doing something. I could hear him rattling around with one of the paintings or sculptures. He was up to something. I don't know... perhaps they had a time limit or something and he changed his mind, but the effort he was going to sounded like he had a task."

"You've got security cameras?"

"Police have asked us to hang onto the files until their investigator can go through copies. I can send them to you if you'd like."

"That would help a lot." I nodded her way. "How are you? This must have been pretty traumatic." Nora was good people, and if she was Nora's friend, Alison probably was, too.

"It's all been happening so fast, to tell you the truth. I haven't even really thought about it," she said. "I suppose I'll probably collapse in a heap of stress at some point, but right now my boss wants me to deal with all of this, so I don't really get a choice."

"Your boss?"

"John DeGoey. He's not exactly what you would call cheerful or easy going."

I knew the name. "Why is he familiar? Where do I know him from?"

"He made a bundle betting against the complex derivatives crew during the economic collapse. Papers covered it."

"Against? That was lucky."

"Okay," she said. "Let's call it that."

"So the gallery… this is a just a hobby for him?"

"Something like that. He has a young trophy wife who likes to dabble in projects. I think this was one of hers at one point, but after it opened she lost interest."

"She doesn't clean up her own messes?"

Pace whistled low and rolled her eyes. "Something like that."

"So he's pretty upset?"

She shrugged. "Wouldn't you be? Even if you guys cover us, our premiums will go through the roof. And the gallery's not exactly what you'd call profitable. She left him with a financial responsibility, but also a social one. Movers and shakers know he owns this place; it has to be successful, safe."

"What's the worst that could happen? He's rich, right? A few people lose faith in his decisions, a few other rich guys make fun of him over a round of golf at Bala."

"He thinks any knock on his rep is dire, because he manages money. That requires his investors' confidence. If he thinks the financial exposure from this is bad enough, he might close the place, I don't know. He's talked about it before, a lot. DeGoey's a wealthy guy but no one gets that way by hanging onto investments that aren't working."

That was true. "What about you?"

"Excuse me?" It caught her off guard. She looked around the museum furtively to see if anyone was listening, unsure what I was suggesting.

"What happens to you if this place closes? Do you have other plans?"

"I look for work, I guess. If you're asking if I have retirement money, you must have already forgotten how much college cost."

"Does that worry you?"

"Sure. But I have good credentials, good references. Good friends like Nora. So… what's in this for you, Liam?"

"I work on commission. If I find your painting, I make a lot of dough. That's a fine incentive to fix problems."

I wasn't going to tell her but I had a little penance of my own to work out still, too; I wasn't sure how I'd managed to con art lovers while displaying such a lack of remorse, and that still frightened me a little bit. When you're worried about the limits of your own poor behavior, life doesn't feel so secure. When you look back and realize you'd fooled yourself into a state of arrogant self-entitlement, the future can look small and daunting.

"That's not much reassurance, but thanks for trying."

"It's not every day we get a case like this."

"Really?"

I smiled. "You'd be surprised how rarely small art galleries are robbed at shotgun point of eight-figure Dutch masters. I mean, I assumed it was a weekly thing, too, but apparently not."

A chuckle. *She has a sense of humor.*

"Did you know everyone else at the show? Anyone stand out or seem out of place in any way?

Her dark eyes were tired, stressed. "Not really. It's an open exhibition, with entry by donation, and most people came earlier in the week. My boyfriend Leo was with me. He's a law student, articling at Walter Beck's firm," Alison said, disappointing the hell out of me and referencing the city's biggest criminal defence lawyer in the same breath.

Walter and I went back a ways.

"The owner of the Vermeer, Paul Dibartolo, was standing by it, talking about it with a local artist, Clinton Dufresne. Dibartolo's new bride is invested in this place, too. I think she and Mrs. DeGoey are old afternoon drinking buds. Dufresne is a really cool customer, a serious soul. Dibartolo had been drinking and Dufresne looked uncomfortable."

I'd seen his name in the trades, the kind of effusive praise that elicited envy and critical interest from other artists, all in one go. "He's a real up-and-comer, I understand."

She gestured at the far wall. "We've had one of his earliest pieces on display, Autumn Mist, for about six months. He came by to ask about a full showing of his other works."

The piece was crooked. "Whoever hung it needs a level," I said.

She frowned. "That's... strange. I suppose it must have happened during the excitement yesterday. Maybe one of the officers brushed against it?" She called over to her assistant. "Stephanie, would you...?"

The younger woman hustled over. "Right away, Alison."

Pace looked over my shoulder for a moment then smiled. "Better. Anyway, Dufresne was talking to Dibartolo at the front of the room. Leo and I were standing just over there by the wall, parallel to the doors. Stephanie was at the front-of-house by the reception desk. DeGoey was by the doors with his wife. He'd been talking to Carl Hecht, who owns the building next door."

"Hecht? What's his story?"

"Hmm... kind of creepy. A schmoozer. A lawyer, I think. He quite obviously wants this building – he's been trying to get DeGoey to sell for years. I know they've dealt with one another before financially, as John doesn't really like him."

"Hecht's law firm is his main business?"

"I don't think so. He has some 'import/export' thing. And he has a couple of other buildings with his brother, so I guess he's into real estate as well."

I took notes and she waited for me to say something, before adding, "Like I said, I imagine everyone will just tell you what they told the police."

"We find it's often helpful to interview witnesses more than once. Brings up inconsistencies and patterns, things that might help, items they forgot the first time around. That sort of thing."

"And have you noticed anything yet?"

"Not really. But maybe the security recordings will give me a better idea of what they were up to."

Alison held out a hand again to shake. My time was obviously up. "Thank you, Mr. Quinn, for your help. I wish I could chat." Her hand was warm.

"Please," I said. "It's Liam. Or just Quinn. Mr. Quinn is my father."

She smiled. "Duly noted, Quinn."

Damn. I was hoping she'd go with Liam.

4.

Alison forwarded everything they'd given the police to the office, along with the security files. But before I headed back to my desk to go through it, I drove south to Chester, a working-class suburb and home to PPL Park, along with the soccer club's offices.

The stadium seats eighteen thousand, a rectangular expanse of concrete and glass with a giant jumbotron screen at one end and open-sided bleachers. It was nestled along the shoreline, the bridge towering over it. It was also about the only thing within five-square miles built since the end of the Vietnam war.

It was also about the only thing within five square miles that looked like it hadn't been through the Vietnam war.

As for the cases of beer, Mike had a point: it was pretty small potatoes to waste our time chasing a booze heist around. But the file had been opened, which meant someone had to close it.

The club's security director was a friendly former military guy named Terence Bryson, a mid-Forties ex-drill sergeant with a short, clipped moustache. He met me at the staff gate, just off the near-empty parking lot.

"Let me show you where the beer was stored," he'd said, leading me along a tall-narrow concrete corridor to a small back room with a single loading dock door. "There had been three young guys working up until about an hour before the robbery. They were is this area, preparing for the game the next day."

PMI wasn't the club's biggest insurer, just a subsidiary policy holder. But Ramon's family was of Spanish extraction, and he loved the sport, too. He called it football, like my dad.

They both moved over in the Sixties from Europe, so they had that in common. They'd worked in precincts on opposite sides of the city and rarely met in the neighborhood, even though Nora and I went to school together for years.

"Why so hot on this? I understand it's a simple theft, a dozen kegs taken?"

"One of our business partners was short the next day for beer in his company's luxury box, for one, which sets a bad example. And the fans went without as well," said Bryson. "Beyond that, we figured since our premiums paid for your investigation, we might as well take advantage and make sure none of the young guys working for us that night were involved."

But he had a look that said that wasn't it. "That all?" I asked.

Bryson chewed his lower lip for a split-second then opened up. "Honestly? I've been a security expert for twenty years, and none of my employers have ever been hit. This is the best job I've ever had, and they're great to work for. I'm not going to let that be ruined."

I didn't need to ask him why they hadn't just called the cops. Even with a break-in, the case would be "warehoused" – stored on a metaphorical high shelf, where it didn't have to take time away from priority investigations, things involving public safety or great financial loss. Recently, the department had taken heat for not showing up at home-invasion-style burglaries until nearly an hour after they'd happened; this didn't even warrant a look, by comparison.

"Can you get me a couple of tickets for the next game?" The Union were playing Toronto that weekend in a battle for second place in the East. "I'll snoop around some, assuming the same crew is working?"

"Sure. We can comp you for as long as you need. Just meet me at the office a half-hour before kickoff. What are you thinking?"

I said, "I'll play it by ear, but there's usually an inside connection on this sort of thing. It'll be kids, probably. They had to hear where the beer was from someone, had to know when to hit it."

"Then you figure it was to drink it, not sell it?" He said it with a twinkle in his eye. We were both teenagers once.

"Maybe a bit of both. It's a lot of beer; might be tough to get them to roll over on each other."

"Over to you, chief," he said.

"Hey, worst come to worst, I get to go to the game," I said.

"You're a fan?"

"Yep. Caught four last year, one so far this year."

"You don't have season seats?"

I shook my head. "Just one of those things. I'm still planning on it, though." I didn't tell him the likelihood of my attending was down to my season-ticket holding brother, Mike, and his current level of irritation with yours truly. Or that I owed any disposable income to the court.

Bryson sighed. "Better sooner than later, chief. They're a hot draw these days."

He had a point. The Union was about the only reason for me to go to Chester, I figured. When the crowd roared and the Sons of Ben sang with full voice, it sure beat just watching the game on TV. Maybe I could cap the experience off by helping them catch a thief.

5.

I don't know why I felt the need to go over to my parents' old neighborhood after meeting with the stadium security expert. Perhaps it was the reminder at the gallery, earlier in the day, that I'd strayed a long way from my roots, both as an artist and as a decent human being.

Or maybe it was just that gnawing sensation I'd get when I was expecting my mother to call and ask why I didn't visit more often.

I avoided the family home, however, and just walked around instead. After about twenty minutes, I found myself standing outside a familiar stucco building, two businesses, with one on each floor. It was the building I'd rented for my first studio, the place at which I'd been "discovered" by my mentor in the world of forgery.

In its back room, I'd dissected the works of multiple schools and multiple artists; Yokoyama Taikan, Gensou Okuda, Shibata Zeshin; I'd used the finest brush points to mimic the former's minute, precise strokes, trying to recapture his esthetic view of picturesque mountain scenes and elegant cranes; I learned to blend colors precisely, like the beloved ochre and reds of Okuda's landscapes. I learned the self-control and restraint required to work in the simple-yet-profound manner of Zeshin.

When you've developed an obsession, it's usually easier for people on the outside to spot your problem, to tell you it's time to back off or get help. But when you're addicted to art? No one sees that as a bad thing. It's just too damn refined. If you drink too much coffee or eat too much junk food, someone will tell you about it. If you spend hours studying paint whorls in Japanese classics? They just think you're a geek.

It took eighteen months of intense study and concentration to reach a point at which my work would fool even the most avid supporter, but it was eventually that good. And I'd revelled in it, in the long, languid hours that passed while working on the tiniest detail; it was as precise as boxing, but with none of the speed, the frenetic ferocity.

From the particle board over the main window, it looked like maybe the place hadn't had a tenant since my move uptown, a year before I went to prison. Even though the neighborhood was humming, it was as if my acts of selfishness had scarred it permanently, left it unwanted.

And that had me thinking about the DeGoey theft: when a gallery has a handful of small-but-expensive classic artists on display, why would a robber ignore them? Each was worth in the tens of thousands, even hot. So why would someone grab the Vermeer but not those? Sure, it was retirement dough if they could move it on the black market. But that was a big if.

And most crooks I know? They don't leave money on the table.

So there had to be more to it than just a robbery.

Assumption number one: the guys who hit the place were working for someone else, being paid as muscle and not in on the main score. If they were, they'd have gotten greedy, gone for other works.

Assumption number two: they were all old pros. A deal that big would mean people with confidence in each other's abilities. If two were just muscle but knew the third, they probably worked together on other jobs or did time together. That made it less likely one of Alison Pace's society friends was calling the shots.

I looked back down the street, towards the bend in the

road. The Druid, an Irish pub favored by cops for decades, was just out of view. My father was probably there, or had been recently. My brother Davy, also a serving member, might be there after his late shift. I went to high school just a few blocks outside the neighborhood. Smoked my first illegal cigarette three streets north of here, behind the old shoe repair shop that used to be there.

There was nowhere on Earth I knew better, and nowhere on Earth that knew me better right back. But even home doesn't feel welcome when you get out of the joint; when everything has gone wrong and nothing you do seems to make it right, even the biggest city can seem like a lonely place.

6.

MY FAMILY'S NEIGHBORHOOD is called Fishtown, and it's about as glamorous as it sounds.

The narrow old brick-and-wood buildings are attached, block-on-block, crammed together tight, tall and skinny, dark hues and wood shingle siding.

Many of them are multi-family and still others – like my parents' house – were simply the most roof that young immigrant families could ever hope to afford back in the day. The streets between them are no wider than modern alleys, with decades of beaten down, repaired and patched asphalt, worn to a near-glassy smoothness in the occasional spot. The city is so old many of them were laid out for carriages originally.

The neighborhood has been filled for years by the ranks of the blue-collar working man: firefighters, cops, dock workers, construction workers, garbage men, mailmen and mall kiosk workers, teachers and transit drivers, all crammed in with their wives and husbands and kids and grandparents, like shoes stored in a box one size too small, then piled on top of one another in a corner cupboard.

Nearly everyone here is Irish, or Italian or Russian. But everyone displays their Star-Spangled Banner in some prominent spot on their house. And they mean it, too. Every person here, no matter how well off they've been, has a father or a grandfather who's willing to smack them silly still, and sit them down and lecture them about some bad jawn in the old country, and how they've got it real good now by comparison.

In summer, when the mercury climbs high, the humidity swelters and the sidewalk feels like it might melt; the close quarters can boil over into trouble, with nowhere good for all of that pressure to go, long-time next-door neighbors coming to rapid blows in short, and unsustainable explosions of passion.

But usually, you see the best in people, a kind of hum of activity as they blow off that steam, of guys in football jerseys and long shorts swapping stories on the stoops while sharing a tall boy, and kids playing in the street, hanging around Central Pizza for a slice or a hoagie, maybe cooling off under an open hydrant; it's a real village in the city, if you come from here. And everybody who comes from here comes from somewhere else.

Even though it's gotten a little more upscale in recent years, with musicians and artists enjoying the affordability, people have thought of Fishtown as low rent for years. But that was fine with us.

When you lived here, you at least knew who your neighbors were. My parents, Al and Maureen, raised five kids in one of those tiny houses, with my dad walking a beat for the better part of twenty years and manning a precinct desk job for another ten after that.

My sister Catherine's a pharmaceutical executive in California, and we don't talk much. We didn't give her the easiest time growing up. But the four boys all stayed home, took on good traditional Irish Catholic jobs: my eldest brother Andy is a priest, my youngest brother Davy is a beat cop, like his old man. Brother number two, Michael, is working his way up the ladder with the city workers' union, although like everyone else, we joke that there ain't much real working involved. If you ever saw the state of I-76 in mid-summer, you'd understand the truth in that.

Me? I was supposed to be the boxer, the success story.

I was a silver gloves champ as a teenager. I got into it two years earlier than most, in a town where a fast set of hands – whether in the ring or through the strike zone – can carry you far. People here, they don't have much sometimes. The 'Rocky' type stories of kids making it from nothing really mean something to folks as a result.

And you want to do it, for them, for supporting you. But in hindsight, that sense of responsibility became a weight around my neck, like trying to keep the world's largest family happy. Everyone in the neighborhood expected me to be an athlete and had decided my future before I'd even thought about it.

In the end, I loved to get away from them all, to find quiet places where I could read or draw. I should have – would have – paid more attention in class if I hadn't been doodling or drawing constantly, or trying to figure out a world no one else could see. My friends thought I was nuts, I think.

When I discovered girls and started rebelling against my parents, my boxing career really went south, a victim of teenage time management. Half out of desperation, my Pa let me attend the Pennsylvania Academy of Fine Arts after high school; it has a world-class rep; but it wasn't what he thought of as a manly kind of thing to do.

That decision and all my stupid choices that followed played frequent roles in our conversations.

I was hoping he wasn't in the mood to go a round or two when I stopped by The Druid.

It was his favorite watering hole, a corner draught bar just off Marlborough Street that had long been a hangout of local Irish Americans and a fair cut of the Philly police department as well. It was hallowed ground, a safe-haven, the kind of place where they never had to hear crap about what goes on behind the blue shield. In the Druid, the good guys were never the bad guys, criminals were all derived from the same ethnicity – scumbag – and modern ideas about diet, feminism and civil rights pretty much went out the window.

Depending on my mood, it felt like a second home.

Its walls were lined with black-and-white photos of Philly lore. Shibe Park, the first local pro ball diamond, long torn down, a rebar-and-concrete pillbox built before the first war; Mike Schmidt teeing off on Mr. Spalding, driving it upper deck; Chuck "Concrete Charlie" Bednarik, the greatest tackler who ever played in the NFL, posing with a ball back in the Fifties; Norm Van Brocklin after beating the Packers back in Nineteen Sixty.

As you might have guessed from the age of the display, it wasn't exactly a happening, trendy spot; the red velour upholstery was even older than the customers.

My father had his own regular stool along the half-hexagon rosewood bar, just in front of an impressive line of draught taps. There was another embroidered seat on one side of him reserved for Davy, and the spot on the other side for Michael. Andy didn't drink so much, except on special occasions. I didn't get a stool, not no more. In fact, most of the time I got the sense I wasn't welcome, at least from the younger regulars. When I walked in, they'd give me long, hard looks, the kind of stares a shopkeep might offer a potential sneak thief.

But I made the effort anyway, because ... well, because it's family, and that's what you do.

My brothers were nowhere to be seen, which was a good thing. Michael wasn't such a problem, but Davy was still taking grief over me at his station over having an ex-con for a brother. We'd gotten along real good when we were kids. He'd looked up to me, the big brother who wasn't so old that we couldn't hang out and goof off.

That's not the kind of relationship that bares up well to a sense of betrayal.

The fact that I'd reformed, landed a respectable job? It

wasn't cutting much slack with him. He wouldn't have believed me, but I understood it; I was at least as ashamed of myself as he was of me.

"What's up kid?" Pa asked as I sidled into Michael's spot. He had a Salisbury steak on the bar counter in front of him and had already demolished about half of it. "You working hard, or hardly working?"

"Hey Pa, how's the battle?"

"Can't complain. Dickie Marshall retired last week and his old lady's already driving him crazy, so he's coming down for a pint. Says he's going to start hanging out here days."

"Someone else for the crib games."

He thought about that. "You know... that's a hell of an idea. He's one lousy crib player, and he's a bad gambler, too. I could use a little extra cash."

Marty was the big, elderly bartender/owner. He knew everybody who drank here regularly going back forty years, but he never said much, even if he knew you well. He was big and he stooped a little, like he had a slight hunchback. His face was narrow, nose thin and birdlike, with the haunted look of a man who understands the world in which he lives.

He brought me over a Rolling Rock – another reason I wasn't too popular with some regulars. I looked at the green beer bottle, its imprinted white label. It had been years since they moved Rolling Rock's production to Jersey, but some of the locals still swore they'd never drink it again. That kind of loyalty, to a product, that seemed like some kind of garbage to me.

Marty said, "You keeping out of trouble, kid?"

I tipped the bottle in his direction and took a swallow. "Pounding the pavement, making a buck. How about you, Marty?"

He waved both hands and leaned on the bar for a moment, fatigued. "Bah. You know how it is, kid. Economy's too rough for me to retire just yet. What I really need is another set of hands around here, but nobody wants a half-time job no more. You got that insurance gig still? You feel like tending bar some weekends?

"I saved the company a hundred grand just this morning, which puts me one step closer to having a mortgage again. And… that's a hard pass on the beer slinging."

My father took another big mouthful of Salisbury steak and got halfway through it before cocking a glance sideways. "A hundred grand? So you get, what… twenty-five hundred? Lunch is on the kid today."

I wasn't going to argue. Technically, seventy percent of that money went directly and immediately from my account to the courts, to pay my outstanding fines, which, as previously noted, were freaking massive. I not only owed my old man, big time, I wanted to give him good reasons to be proud for the first time since my college graduation.

He finished up, sponging the remaining gravy with a dinner roll, before centering his cutlery. Then he finished the second half of his glass of beer. "Another Straub, Marty," he said. Straub was hard-core local beer; a German-style brew produced in small batches by an old family outfit in St. Mary's, a small town up in the northwest of the state.

My old man loved it, even though he was Irish as they come. It was either Guinness or Straub, and nothing else.

He nodded towards the patio. "Let's go stand outside for a minute so I can have a smoke without offending anyone else's delicate sensibilities." Even though he'd beaten prostate cancer when he was younger, my old man still went through a half-pack of Winston a day. We'd all long given up trying to change his mind.

Well… everyone except Ma.

Outside the front door, Pa took a deep drag and blew out the smoke. "So what's up kid? You never come around this time of day. Is that fancy new condo of yours downtown feeling lonely?"

I was renting a nice one-room loft just off the arts district until I could put a down payment on my own place. "No, I just wanted to stop in when I had a chance," I said, checking out the busy street traffic, noisy in the late afternoon. "Look, I've got a big case to work on; not sure I'm going to make it over for Sunday dinner."

He shot me a dead stare. "You want me to tell your mother? I don't think so. You're skipping her Sunday dinner? You call her up and tell her. You were gone for near on four years. The idea isn't going to sit well, Liam. Jaysus, the last time I didn't hear the end."

"You talk to Davy yet?" I tried to say it nonchalantly, like my little brother's opinion of me wasn't a big deal. Like it didn't hurt like Hell when he made it clear how I'd let him down.

Pa looked down at his shoes. "So: that's what you're really worrying about."

I nodded. "Yeah. You know it is."

"Look, you just got to give him time, Liam. He needs to get past it in his own way, like the rest of us."

"You ain't past it neither. None of you are. That much is pretty clear, most days."

"Should I be? Should any of us?"

I looked down at the pavement, feeling the shame again. "No, course not. I know how bad I messed up, believe me. I did the time."

He blew out a turbulent cloud of blue smoke "We all did the time."

"Yeah." I knew that, too.

"Well, it's just going to be harder for Davy, that's all. He's got to work with guys you both grew up around."

"So… you've talked to him?"

He shook his head. "No. But if you're not coming over on Sunday, I'm sure the topic of your job over the last year will come up. Your mother will raise it, if nothing else."

"She's the best."

"Better than either of us deserve. Hell of a lot better. So...what's the case?"

"Art gallery robbery yesterday, Center City. A Vermeer."

I regretted the words as soon as they left my mouth, and sure enough, he looked at me cockeyed again.

"That supposed to mean something to me?"

"Old dead Dutch guy."

"So... worth a lot of money, then."

"Yeah, a ton. Millions."

He hated that I liked art, that I saw more in it than he did. Maybe it was just old Irish resentment; Ma had always enjoyed a pretty oil or landscape and she'd painted a few still life works of her own, although admittedly without success. But Pa had never understood it or seen much in it. I think he was a bit embarrassed by it all.

"You couldn't just be a bank robber, like Pavel's youngest boy." He didn't say it with a wry lilt or anything; he wasn't kidding. He didn't like crooks, but at least he understood them.

Pavel Yashin was our Russian Orthodox neighbor. His best friend, Lev Manovsky, had been my father's partner for about a year until hypertension forced Mr. Manovsky onto a desk.

My dad figured Pavel got jealous of them being friends right about then. Ever since, he and dad competed over everything.

"Being a safe cracker would be better than forging?"

He snorted. "Cop has a grudging respect for a safe cracker. That's an old-school criminal, right there. But who wants a painter in the family?" He tossed his cigarette down onto the roped off sidewalk that substituted for a "patio" at The Druid. "Well, your mother's not going to be happy, so you'll hear about it next week. But at least you get out of church, too."

"You got that right. Just let her know I couldn't avoid it, okay? It's a work thing."

He smiled and clapped a hand on my shoulder. "You figure out a way to get me out of it too, you let me know."

I didn't have the heart to tell him that I kind of enjoy church. I'd already shattered any illusions he'd held about being a jock. Liking church would forever mark me as weak-willed to Dad and Davy, even as they told everyone how proud they were of Andy. They were always scheming to get out early and watch football.

It was one thing to be a priest; a local neighborhood priest could still command some respect, even with the troubles the church was facing. But admitting you liked church? Well, that was like admitting you enjoyed missing the pre-game show.

Dad had his priorities figured out. If he could get out of church, he would. He'd still pray, of course – but it usually had something to do with the Eagles and whether they'd beat the point spread.

7.

I had to guess Leo Tesser came from money. For a law student who presumably had big bills to pay, he sure lived in a trendy spot.

Alison Pace's fiancé had a condo that was part of a neat old factory conversion off Broad Street and Lehigh Avenue. It was the kind of immaculate old dark-brick structure that could have doubled for a set on a TV show in which young people shared their hilarious life problems.

She'd called ahead to tell him I was coming. I parked the Beast under a shade tree outside so the cracked-leather seats wouldn't suffer.

I was about to cross the street when a short blonde woman walked out of the building. She was beautiful, her hair pushed up in a flowing ponytail, white blouse, short blue skirt, white stockings, and tall heels with seductive ankle straps. She couldn't have been more than five-feet-two.

She stopped outside the building for a moment and looked around before striding confidently down the street, turning more than a few male heads along the way but not even registering it herself, as accustomed to the attention as to breathing. Then she crossed over to a green Acura, unlocking the door from ten feet away with a remote. A few seconds later, she was gone.

I waited for a few cars to pass then walked over to the brownstone and up its four front steps to the buzzer board. Leo was in 4A.

"Hello?"

"Mr. Tesser? It's Liam Quinn, from Philadelphia Mutual."

"Hi, yeah, Alison called. Just a second."

The door buzzer fired, one of the old ones that you had

to catch just in time. Four green linoleum steps led up to the first floor then twisted to the right, parallel to the dirty cracked plaster wall, continuing up three flights to the dimly lit corridor outside Leo's apartment.

His place was at the other end of the hall. I was about to knock when the door opened. Leo swung it ajar casually. He only had jeans on, plus a towel draped over his shoulders. "Come on in, Mr. Quinn. Sorry, she didn't give me much notice and I was just taking a shower."

The apartment was as old as the corridors suggested, with narrow-plank hardwood floors, high skirting boards and a small, separate kitchen near the front door. I thought I caught a whiff of perfume coming in. Past the entry corridor was a cramped living room, with big windows that looked out onto the alley behind the building.

Leo was a good-looking young guy, with tousled black locks. He walked over to the couch and grabbed a t-shirt, which he pulled on quickly. He rubbed at his wet hair with the small towel. "I only have a couple of hours before I have to get back to the firm for a meeting."

His internship with Walter Beck. Walter and I had run into each other plenty over the years.

"Yeah, Alison mentioned you were over there. How is old Walter, anyway?" I probably didn't need to ask. Walter always looked after Walter, first and foremost.

He threw the towel onto the coffee table and chuckled. "About the same as ever. Never saw a retainer he didn't like or a guy who didn't deserve a defense."

"Hey, I've heard that story before. My old man? He'd have a problem with it."

Leo smiled. "Mine too."

"You from Philly?"

"Chicago, southwest of downtown. Tough neighborhood."

"Yeah, we got those here." Then I remembered South Chicago was mostly black neighborhoods and felt a flush of white privilege guilt. By 'those' I hadn't meant…

Never mind.

He motioned for us to sit down in the living room. "You want a coffee or a juice or something?"

"Sure, black with one sugar?"

He leaned his head out the door while prepping the coffee. "So any particular reason Alison thought I could help?"

"Nah, I'm just being thorough."

"Ah." He didn't sound convinced. "That doesn't sound like her. She's normally on point." He ducked back into the kitchen.

His place was spartan but well-loved. He had a couple of French impressionist prints in nice frames, a Lalique-style statuette on the old fireplace. On the far wall were his graduation certificates. Apparently, Leo Tesser's government-issued handle was "Leonard Albert Tesser-Piddle."

A few moments later he returned with two cups and some sugar in a bowl. Coffee was a luxury inside the joint and I still couldn't help but take advantage whenever someone offered, even though too much caffeine makes my brain shaky. He sat down opposite me, then saw me glance at the certificates. "Yeah… Piddle isn't the greatest surname in the world to begin a career with," he explained. "As a lawyer, Tesser had a nice ring."

"Understood."

"Alison's idea, when we were starting out in school together."

"She took law?"

"We were both taking a BA originally. When she mentioned me… she didn't take any shots at me, nothing personal?"

"Why? Are you two having trouble?"

He looked down, pursing his fingertips together like a nervous kid. He leaned forward a little, tense. "Yeah. It's been tough lately." Then he caught himself moping and straightened up, serious. "You know how it is, relationships."

"Been there, man, been there."

"We were engaged, then we weren't, now I guess we are. So ... she didn't say anything about me?"

"Not really, no."

"Oh." He looked embarrassed. "Well, I feel kind of stupid then. So ... how can I help you, Mr. Quinn?"

I took a sip of my drink then put the cup down on a magazine on his coffee table.

"I just want to go over the day's events again, see if you maybe spotted or remember anything helpful."

"Sure." He crossed his legs anxiously.

"You okay?"

"Yeah, it's ... I'm just still a bit jumpy because of it, you know?" Leo laughed nervously. "I actually slept with the light on last night, if you can believe that stuff. Pretty dumb, right?"

It was the usual reaction after being robbed. "It's normal. There's always a little post-traumatic shock after something that stressful and dangerous. So... the two guys ... tell me what you remember about them."

He thought about it for moment. "Not much to tell, really. They were dressed identically, blue bomber jackets, denim jeans, black army boots."

"Army? You sure?"

"No, no. Not, like, actual Army boots. Just black boots with a high ankle. I'm not sure if they were Army, though."

"Ok, so who was in charge?"

"The little guy, I think. I mean short. He wasn't a dwarf or anything, just shorter. He was the guy who fired the shot into the ceiling when they came in. He went to the front of the room. We were all face down, so I couldn't see exactly what he was doing, but I assume that's when the Vermeer was grabbed."

He'd used the artist's name. "You enjoy Vermeer?"

"He's okay, I guess. To be honest, I can't really tell them apart without Alison whispering crap in my ear about them. Paintings pretty much look alike to me, you know? I think most people buy them for status."

The generic ignorance was irritating, but I let it go.

"And the other guy?"

Leo shook his head. "Don't know. Like I said, I was pretty far forward in the room and he was somewhere behind us, I think maybe guarding the door."

The story was basically the same as Alison's. I needed to check out that security footage.

I asked him how long they'd been dating.

"About fifteen months on the second go around, I guess."

"But it's going badly now?"

He looked ambivalent "I mean, I'm not even sure really. I don't know. We still like each other, I guess."

"You guess But you never saw it as any big serious thing, despite being engaged."

"No, not really. Like I said, we'd been engaged before and broke up. Look, does this have anything to do with the robbery?"

I held up both palms. "Just covering all the bases. I mean, that's why you were there … right?"

He looked guilty for asking the question. "Yeah... sorry. I know you're just doing your job. This whole thing is just, well, it's pretty stressful, you know? I've got cases to work on for Walter and I still need to shop for a job when this is all done."

"If you think I'm tough, you're going to face a lot more scrutiny if you go to work for Walter," I said. "Some of the doozy defenses he's come up with over the years are legendary."

"That's not going to happen, though. He only has one associate and the man is in his forties and happy; he's not going anywhere. It's unfortunate. Walter bills big hours. He's no friend to the average lawman. I don't think there's a crook left in Philly he hasn't represented."

"So... are you going down that path?"

He shrugged. "I don't know yet. Everybody deserves a good defence."

"Everybody?"

"Only way the system works."

"I guess." I wouldn't have wanted him to repeat that around my old man. After a few years of watching scumbags get off or get slaps on the wrist, he'd become leery of social reform and the parole system.

He shrugged. "It's true. For now, it's just a great place to article. Big cases, plenty of research, plenty of chance to make a name – I mean, he's been on the front page three times in the last nine months, and I've been standing behind him twice. That can help a career. He does a lot of civil cases, too, so there's choice."

I finished my coffee then got out a business card and handed it to him. "Do me a favor: you think of anything else, you call me on that number. It's also good for the odd favor."

He smiled and extended a hand to shake. "Careful: I might take you up on that."

I smiled politely and didn't ask him about the woman who'd just left, or the lingering scent of her perfume. As I turned to look back at his apartment while crossing the road to my car, a curtain fell back into place, across the window.

8.

Sometimes truth is stranger than fiction. You spend enough time with police in your family, you hear about every kind of weird robbery, fraud or homicide. And in most cases, the robberies featured someone on the inside, connected to the business or home that got hit.

It's usually how the bad guys know there's something to be taken in the first place.

That meant taking the time to visit everyone Alison had managed to identify as attending, even though I was pretty sure my next stop didn't need the money or grief a heist would present.

Paul Dibartolo's mansion was in Chestnut Hill, a greenery-laden elderly neighborhood in northwest Philly. People around here had money as old as the giant oaks and ash. With that money came the kind of power that backed candidates all the way to Washington, or made problems disappear without attracting attention and notoriety; they were robber barons of the online age, mixed with the grandchildren of their turn-of-the-century equivalents, all packed in next door to crooked venture capitalists and big corporate dreamers.

Everything in the zip code cost a mint. Some of the homes were understated; but others here were monstrous, foreboding concrete monuments with wrought iron fences, circular driveways that could accommodate the limousines of heads of state, and clocks that chimed like Big Ben.

Somber house staff members were always nearby, dinner came in five or more courses, and the familiar crackle of a parking lot's perfect gravel under tires was a reminder of the sheer opulence of it, of owning a home with a lot bigger than a city block, of marble floors and chandeliered ballrooms.

I could practically hear the Handel score kicking in as I found a parking spot for my piece-of-crap Firebird, eight feet away from a silver-grey Aston Martin that cost more than my parents' house.

At the top of the concrete steps, a butler in long tails was waiting to greet me. "Mr. Dibartolo will see you in his study, sir. If you would follow me..."

He led me down a long marble-floored hallway. To the left were a series of enormous rooms, each exposed through giant double doors, towering ceiling mouldings above over the kind of antique furniture you only saw in museums – and joints like Paul Dibartolo's house. To the right, the wall featured a series of portraits, presumably of family.

At the end was a large oaken door. He knocked twice gently then listened attentively with one ear to it.

"Enter," said a voice I assumed belonged to Dibartolo.

He opened the door and held it for me. "Mr. Liam Quinn, sir, of the Philadelphia Mutual Insurance Company."

The man behind the desk was rotund, with messy silver-grey hair and a pair of half-glasses perched low on his bulbous nose. "Thank you, Ripley. If you could bring some tea and coffee for our guest..."

Ripley bowed and exited, closing the door behind him. The study fit the rest of the house. At one end, a gigantic black onyx fireplace dominated, and in front of the three large bay windows Dibartolo sat behind an oversized Rosewood desk. The walls were lined with tall bookcases, and the carpet was thick shag, plush under my feet like an uncut lawn.

"Mr. Quinn."

"Sir. So, that's... that's Ripley, huh?"

"Indeed. A good man."

"He's changed a lot since *Alien,* gotten less shapely."

"He's... Oh. Ripley, like the woman. Yes, quite amusing. I understand you've been charged by the insurance men with the task of trying to recover my painting." He was tough to read, dispassionate.

"I'm investigating the theft, yes. I was hoping you might be able to give me some insight, as one of the people there at the time."

His voice had an edge of fatigue. "I'm not easily intimidated. I was in Vietnam, as you may be aware if you've read my biography. But I have to admit the whole thing put me on edge."

"Ms. Pace at the gallery indicated you'd extended the loan of the picture to save on the insurance costs."

"You get right to the point, Mr. Quinn. Admirable."

"It saves everyone time."

He tilted his head back slightly as if pondering his answer. "Sure, I can appreciate that. As you can see," he motioned around us, "it's not a case of needing the money."

"But you like the painting. You'd have kept it here if you didn't loan it to the gallery?"

"Sure, maybe. I don't know really, Mr. Quinn. To be truthful I didn't think that much about it at all. Let's just say it was mutually beneficial."

"Your accountant's idea?"

"Mine."

"You get that involved in the day-to-day?"

"I wouldn't be rich if I didn't. That painting cost me $2.3 million more than two decades ago. You can imagine what it might be worth now. With a little word-of-mouth from the show, I could've had the old money in town or in New York bidding five times that. Maybe more. The insurance settlement won't replace it, or make me as much."

The butler re-entered with a silver serving tray and set about preparing us each a cup. I said, "I noticed you don't seem to have any other staff working. This is a pretty huge place for just one extra set of hands."

He nodded but didn't say anything. After a moment, he added, "Was there a question in there, Mr. Quinn? Perhaps an implication?"

"So the economy's not hitting you? I mean, if I'm sitting on six thousand square feet of mansion in Chestnut Hill, you better believe I've got more than one guy helping me out."

"The economy's hitting everybody. That doesn't mean I'm in trouble."

It wasn't much of an answer. "But you're not trying to find extra sources of cash? Ways to save?"

He licked his lips tensely. "Okay, sure, things have been a bit tough at the office lately. We've consolidated a little. Our holdings on the east coast aren't meeting expectations.."

"Have they been tough enough to warrant hiring a crew to rip off your own painting? The gallery takes the insurance hit, you'd still get to sell the painting, get paid twice."

He gave me a surprised stare that suggested the idea was ridiculous. "Really? For a few million you think I'd risk everything I have? And as I'm sure you know from personal experience, on the black market it wouldn't fetch a fraction of market value."

I'd been looking around his office as we spoke, trying to get a picture of the guy beyond the obvious preconceptions and stereotypes about wealth. His comment about what I'd know snapped me out of it. "You looked me up."

"As I said, I wouldn't be much of a businessman. I remember your gallery, actually. Very trendy for a while. I'm glad I didn't get taken."

"And yet you're talking to me anyway."

He shrugged. "Business is business."

He had a couple of university degrees on the wall; the books verged towards non-fiction, a few from the cult-ofpersonality end of the spectrum. On the fireplace mantle was a picture of his wife and kids.

"You've got two boys?" They both looked around high school age.

He nodded. "Picture's a few years old. They're both grown now."

Alison had mentioned his date to the gallery show. "Divorced?"

Another nod. "Yeah, for about a decade."

"Paying alimony?"

Dibartolo snorted. "Through the nose. Price of freedom, I guess. Look, I have a lot of work to do, Mr. Quinn. I'm not sure I can add anything to help you. I can tell you I didn't have anything to do with this, since that's what you seem to be getting at."

"If I'm in your spot, Mr. Dibartolo, I'm not sure how helpful I'd be. You're going to do pretty well off this settlement."

He shrugged. "I usually do."

"What about the two men? Anything you remember about them?"

He thought it over. "The big one, who walked behind us towards the back of the room – I think he removed one of the paintings. It sounded like it, anyway."

"Sounded like it?"

"A scratching noise followed by the sound of him putting something on the floor, then a scratching noise again, maybe the clatter of the frame against the wall."

"You weren't paying attention to the guy at the front of the room?"

"The shotgun blast seemed designed to focus attention on him."

"And everyone else did. Why not you?"

9.

Dibartolo smiled warmly and spread both palms wide, as if to demonstrate just how open he was willing to be. "Would you like me to express remorse at not being sufficient terrified as to be rendered witless, Mr. Quinn?"

"But like you said, a shotgun blast is a hell of a distraction..."

"When you work in finance, Mr. Quinn, you learn to look out for sleight-of-hand. You learn to look for the signal, rather than be distracted by loud noises. I'm not fond of being robbed at gunpoint, but the crooks you face in the financial world can be infinitely more dangerous, if only for their relative subtlety."

"Uh huh. But fear is fear..."

"Spend eighteen weeks in the jungle with little relief, with bullets fired at you every time you turn around, with buddies sniped feet away, with everything out there in the dark able to eat you or kill you... No, Mr. Quinn. I don't scare easily."

"Anything else strike you?"

He took a deep breath, exhaling slowly. "DeGoey. John. He was calm, calmer than I would have expected. Everyone else looked terrified; he looked... aware. Like he was watching something moving on schedule."

"It stood out that much to you?"

"Well... certainly, yes. Perhaps I'm conflating my preexisting biases with what I actually saw. He may just have a military background as well, or policing or something. But..."

"But?"

"I mean, he's been having troubles, you know? It's really no secret in the local real estate community. I only know him from the club, really. If I'm honest about it, I thought loaning the painting to his gallery might help his reputation a little. He's got some interesting associates, made some bad choices."

"Are you sure that couldn't be affecting your memory, too, being burned while you thought you were doing him a favor?"

He looked annoyed. His eyes flitted towards the double doors with impatient intent. He'd tried to make the point that he was the ice king and I was still asking him about irritants. That made me one, I guess.

His gaze flitted back from the door to me. Or, through me, really. "My time, as you say, is quite valuable, Mr. Quinn..."

I hit the office one more time before going home for the night. Everyone left at least a half-hour earlier and I had to flick on the bank of neon lights to get around.

At my desk I checked my e-mail and sure enough, the video files from the gallery's security cameras were there, along with a note from Alison Pace.

"Hope this speeds things up."

I downloaded the files then hit play. The angle was from the back corner of the room and clearly displayed about ninety percent of the gallery space. I paused the video when the two guys burst into the room, slamming open the glass front door. Between boxing and forgery I got to know my share of local wise guys and it occurred to me that if I was lucky, I might just recognize the clowns responsible.

No such luck. Both were as nondescript as the various witnesses had described. The camera shook a little when the first guy let off the shotgun blast. Sure enough, the small guy barked a couple of commands to the prone patrons, then moved quickly to the front of the room and grabbed the Vermeer, placing it in a small knapsack. The big guy went to the back of the room … and disappeared from view, obviously standing in the ten percent or so of the room that the camera couldn't pick up.

Damn.

I checked the file from the camera in the opposite corner of the room. It gave me the reverse angle. The big guy stopped in front of the back wall for a few moments; then he took the painting off the back wall, the one that had been crooked when I'd visited. He crouched down for a moment, but his body size obscured what he was up to. Then he hung the picture back up again.

That was a head-scratcher.

A split-second later the guy at the front of the room finished up. They exited together and, after a few appropriately fearful minutes, the gallery manager got up and called the police.

Within a few more moments everyone else had also risen to their feet, their movements full of stress and exhilaration. Dibartolo hugged DeGoey's wife. It took DeGoey, the owner of the gallery who'd been standing nearest the doors, a little longer than most to get up. His wife looked familiar, too, even on the grainy security film.

The stunning blonde with the lilac perfume, coming out of Leo Tesser's building.

It couldn't have been a coincidence. Well … it could have been. But I'm not a big believer.

10.

I wasn't sure what to make of it as I drove over to my apartment. My building was on Ranstead and was nothing special from the outside, just mottled cement and windows that went up for floor after floor. But the apartment itself was nice, a proper loft, with a kitchen cubicle in one area, a living room, and a murphy bed that popped out of a hidden cubby hole in the red-brick wall.

In the back corner I'd hung my heavy bag and speed bag. The large windows on the front of the building provided a nice view while jumping rope or doing push-ups and crunches; and they slid open in summer to keep the heat from building up too much.

The only separate room in the place was the small, functional bathroom, with a shower cubicle in one corner, a sink across the middle of one wall and a toilet in another corner. Not fancy, but it suited my purposes. It wasn't supposed to be permanent. I stopped thinking in terms of permanency the day I went away to serve my time.

But before I could get home, put my feet up and relax a little, I had to park the beast in the building's underground lot. I'd pulled it into its regular slot and was walking to the elevator when a voice behind me called out.

"Hey! Liam!"

It was Ricky Ellis, my neighbor and, as far as I could tell so far, the building's resident good guy.

"What's shaking, Ricky?"

Ricky was as gay as a pride parade, which when you're also from a devoutly religious family can be a Hell of a tough road. Like many in the gay community, he hadn't let it beat him down. Instead, he'd become stronger for it, an outgoing man. A warm person.

He'd been rejected by his family's community and made one of his own instead among the residents in the building, where he helped the older folks, hung out with those of us who had the time or inclination and also met his new boyfriend, a retired school custodian named Al. Al, as far as I could tell, was also a Hell of a nice guy.

"Liam, man, you got to hang around the building more. We had a par-ty here last weekend… all I can say is 'Wow!' Baby, you don't know what you're missing."

I smiled. "I heard. Not really my thing, but I'm glad everyone had a good time. I hear Old Lady Corbett on the first floor was dancing in the hallways."

"Too bad you couldn't make it, my friend. You should have seen the younger ladies! That girl up on the top floor, woo! The college chickie. She like you, man! Oh baby! She's excitable! She kept talking about watching you jog in those long shorts… And you would have been the only straight guy under 40."

"My luck. Had a case."

"We had a case too … a case of wine. At least! I felt, like, poisoned for two days. But here I am, beautiful as ever."

"Ouch. The wine and me… we don't agree on much of anything."

"You know it. My head is still hurting five days later. Wine is a bitch."

"How's Al?"

"Oh, you know. His sciatica's acting up. He says he can tell the fall is coming."

Al was at least twenty years older than Ricky but neither seemed to notice, and once people had been around them together for a few moments, they didn't generally, either.

"My old man's the same way. Trick knee."

"But it's so sexy when Al needs me," he said. "He's like a little baby deer."

"Right. My old man might shoot a little baby deer and eat it. But that's as close as he'd come. Much to our horror when we were kids, he used to crack jokes during the opening of Bambi, when the mom dies."

He laughed. "Oh man, that's awful! Hey... did you get that message?"

"What...?"

"The two guys." My blank look drew elaboration. "Two guys stopped by yesterday, said they might have a job for you."

If I was in the habit of accepting freelance gigs from strangers, it might have made sense. But naturally my alarm bells were going off.

"What'd they look like, Rick?"

He thought about it. "Sloppy dressers, like most middle-aged fat cis men. Suspenders, dress pants, raincoats."

Feds or wiseguys. Or maybe just salesmen. "Were they carrying anything? You know, like Encyclopaedias or anything?"

He shook his head. "No. They just kept their hands in their pockets and said to tell you they stopped by. Oh... and sunglasses. It was lousy outside but they had sunglasses on, aviator style."

The aviators said Feds. But Feds wouldn't have said anything. They'd have just come back later.

I didn't want to worry the kid, so I just nodded and smiled, then headed for elevator. "No big deal. I'm sure they'll catch up to me. Look, I'm going to head upstairs."

"Oh... yeah, okay, man. If you want to stop by for a beer later, Al's making his flatbread pizza. It's really good. You'll really like it, ese."

Ever the host. "I might do, I might do. We'll see how the evening goes."

"Right on, Liam. Later baby," he said, before heading

61

towards his little green Toyota.

Upstairs, I changed into a short-sleeved sweatshirt and shorts and got in a quick workout, before hammering the speed bag for a few minutes, trying to puzzle out what the big guy had been up to with that painting while I built a sweat.

I thought about the photo of the Clinton Dufresne painting that Alison had shown me, its graceful sliding curves and lines, the muted sense of color blooming within its abstract shapes.

I was going to need another look at it.

Once I'd broken a sweat, I took a break, feeling the familiar tightness in my biceps and abdominal external obliques from working the bag. I looked out of the picture window at the city below. The lights and traffic maintained a constant colored blur, even as the evening drew in and the sun hung low in a hazy sky.

Somewhere out there, that Vermeer was my ticket towards paying off my debt and getting back on my feet, and it was waiting for me to find it.

I didn't want to worry Ricky; but now I had the added pressure of keeping my head down, because Philly's a town with a long history of mobsters popping up in the most inconvenient places. It sure sounded like two had paid me a visit, which wasn't good.

And I had to figure out what that stunning blonde was doing sleeping with another guest from the gallery opening, the unfortunately monikered Leonard Piddle, now Leo Tesser. I was damn sure Alison Pace didn't know about it, which begged the question of what else she hadn't been told about that day.

11.

The woman at the courthouse wicket had chatted with

me before on another case. She was older, I'd guess close to retirement, with square glasses and sensible, short hair, and seemed like the amiable type.

She finished stamping pieces of paper with the courthouse seal. "You don't ask for much, do you Liam? You know you can get most of this online now, right?"

The file folder on the counter ahead of her looked about an inch thick. She'd been busy. "Geez, Grace, got much for me, there?"

"Better you than me," she said. "Anyway, the copying's going to cost you thirty-two seventy-five."

I took the weighty folder to a nearby reference desk and sat down with it. One of the things I'd learned about investigative work from Ramon Garcia de Soria is that a lot of it is tedious, and a lot of it involves reading documents drier than a piece of toast in the Sahara.

Before you can start asking people questions and investigating motives, you have to make sure you're questioning the right people and that you're asking the right questions. And that usually means going through paperwork – or at the very least, digital archives. If you don't know a subject well, you can't cover all the bases. If you don't know anything about them, you won't spot the inconsistencies in their statements, the little lies that can reveal big discrepancies.

Most people have no idea how much available information there is on them out there and publicly available: vital statistics, residential records, property ownership and titles, liens, civil and criminal court filings, acknowledgements for donations, online references, library troves of school yearbooks … all of these things help a good investigator track someone down, or trip someone up.

And most of it sticks around forever.

A title search on Paul Dibartolo's Chestnut Hill home,

for example, showed an outstanding mortgage of $2.4 million from a new lien issued just six months earlier. But he'd bought it on a lien four years before that, which meant this was a second mortgage, and big one at that – almost as much as he'd originally paid for the house.

He also had a sealed civil settlement with his first wife. Lots of civil documents – usually those from family court – weren't considered public information. But a handful of the other suits mentioned the value of the spousal support payments, and he was keeping her in a fine style.

A few other civil suits seemed to involve partners and suppliers, not uncommon for someone of Dibartolo's affluence. They added up to a couple of million dollars more.

Still, I had a hard time picturing Dibartolo laying down the law to hired muscle. That mortgage bill was big enough to warrant all sorts of action, but guys like him? They didn't usually hire a couple of hard men to knock over a gallery. It just wasn't the right style. Rich guys used other people's money to leverage more of other people's money – it's why they're always reinventing themselves.

No, Dibartolo was probably a thief, of a sort; very few guys with that sort of money and that sort of debt were straight-laced. But I couldn't see him pulling the heist. Finance guys liked to work within the constraints of what could be debated as legal after the fact, at the very worst.

This kind of logic, of course, is not something my father and brother would agree with; they're old school policemen, flatfoots. They know that ninety-eight percent of the time, the first guy who looks like he did it, did it.

Most of the crimes they dealt with were just that simple. If it looks like a duck, quacks like a duck and kills people like a duck, it's probably the duck you're looking for; so arrest the duck.

The kind of guys they ran into – neighborhood low-lifes

and operators – weren't big on subtlety and were tripped up easily. They were guys with poor impulse control, tempers, immaturity and emotional imbalance.

The Philly police still routinely picked up guys wanted on warrants by sending them an invite to a free raffle draw, for example. Sometimes, the pickup rate for what had to be the dumbest sting in history was as high as eight-five percent. At another one, they offered to forgive credit card debt for anyone wanted on warrants. More than eight hundred guys showed up.

The all-time Mac Daddy was the 'yacht giveaway'. I kid you not. Forty-two felons actually thought they were just being given a yacht. So when you're talking about the criminal underworld, don't ever mix up 'shrewd' and 'cunning' with intelligent. The former two are based on animal instinct, and they had plenty, usually. The latter required critical thinking and was often lacking or never really brought into play.

This case was different. It may have been that a couple of sides of beef pulled it off; but I doubted the two guys on the camera were fans of obscure Dutch painters.

Of course, Dibartolo wasn't the only person there during the robbery with major moolah. The gallery owner, John DeGoey, had a court civil file that made Dibartolo's look economically optimistic.

He was facing civil suits – and a number of outstanding judgments – from dozens of companies. Some of the awards were huge, in the low millions of dollars. The gallery building, meanwhile, was strictly floating on bank paper. Why the bank hadn't sued yet to try to minimize its exposure or seize the asset I couldn't say, but it was surprising.

The third big-money guy there was the next-door neighbor, Carl Hecht. A large, beefy man with pale skin, thinning sandy hair and glasses, Hecht's building was owned by a numbered company, free and clear. A corporate registration search on the company showed Hecht as one of the directors. Its address was another building downtown.

Typically, these addresses led to the company's legal counsel, and the three law firms listed at the other building confirmed that was likely the case. On a hunch, I ran a title search on the law office, and it was owned by the same numbered company.

The suggestion was that Carl Hecht had a heck of a lot of money. But it was of the anonymous, corporate persuasion – and that always makes me nervous. Taking on individuals, especially those operating on the shady side of the law, was one thing. Taking on the full legal might of a modern corporation was a hell of a lot more intimidating. A biker will try to punch your lights out and, if you're lucky, won't stomp you so hard afterwards that he kills you. But a big corporation will destroy your life, your hopes and your dreams accidentally, without even noticing, and still won't give a damn afterwards.

Imagine what one can do when it's really going after you.

I gathered up the photocopied documents and shoved them pack into the folder then set off for the parking lot and the Beast. I was a few feet outside the courthouse doors when the voice sounded behind me.

"Yeah... I might've figured I'd find you here – either digging up dirt on my case or being arraigned. Never up to any good, usual."

I turned, making sure I was smiling. "And how are you this fine morning, Detective Trevanian?"

He looked pissed. He was scowling, hands clenched in fists, probably without even realizing he was doing it. "You're some kind of pain in my ass, you know that, right, Quinn?"

"What is it this..."

"You're stepping all over my investigation, riling up witnesses, upsetting important citizens..."

"I didn't tell your cousin to buy the stupid painting, Bill..."

"It's *detective* to you, convict. Our families stopped being friends when you done what you done. Now I hear you're interviewing people at the gallery, bothering Paul Dibartolo. Don't you think it's bad enough, what you done? Now you have to act like you're not from a family of police, and you didn't betray all of us? Your brother, the poor bastard, he's never going to live it down! And he's a good cop..."

"Look, I did my time..."

"Sure. And I bet you had a real heartfelt change inside, or you found Jesus or some other crap, some other excuse that'll disappear out the window like someone else's money as soon as it's convenient. We'll be busting your ass and putting you back inside within a year. Mark my words."

"I haven't done anything..."

He wasn't hearing it. He interrupted me again, stabbing a finger through the air to enunciate his stance. "Stay away from my case, Quinn. Or so help me, I'll put your ass back in Curran-Fromhold myself."

He shoved past me, our shoulders colliding. Trevanian yanked the library doors open angrily and tromped inside.

12.

I'd anticipated needing to talk to DeGoey and Hecht after my initial conversation with Alison Pace, and put calls in to both to try to set something up.

I still hadn't heard from the latter, but DeGoey had a few free minutes on Friday morning. I was going to take advantage, even though I still had Trevanian's bitching in my ear. The notion of ignoring his less-than-polite demands and bugging one of his witnesses within a few minutes of his tirade was too appealing to turn down.

His office was on the twelfth floor, with tall tinted windows that looked out over the city. DeGoey was a ginger-haired man with a wispy beard, seated behind an expansive, modern desk with a glass-insert top; he was leaning back in his leather office chair with his legs crossed and fingertips together, like a talk show host studying his guest.

One of the things I learned quickly from Ramon is that it helps to interview a man in his own surroundings. It affords him a false sense of ease and confidence. It also gives you a chance to inspect those surroundings for information: where he went to school, whether he has pictures of his family, what kind of stuff he reads.

It may sound trivial, but by the end, you have at least a small idea of who the guy really is, and when it comes to asking questions that he'll answer, that's a real advantage.

His office was just a few blocks away from the gallery and I made a mental note to find out how much he owed on it. If his financial problems on the gallery building were any indication – not to mention the number of people suing him – the place had to be hocked up to the rafters.

But for now, DeGoey was playing the role of the

bewildered host.

"I was quite surprised when you called to say you'd be dropping by," he said.

"Really?"

"I can't understand how much simpler this could be, Mr. Quinn. Surely everything the police gathered on the day gave you enough information..."

"In what respect, sir?"

"To make a decision on..."

"That's not really my...

"To make a decision our claim," he finished. "You are with PMI, are you not?"

"Yes, but I'm just the initial investigator, on the circumstances leading up to the claim."

"Well, our premiums were fully up-to-date, yes?"

"To my knowledge, sir, yes, there's no issue there."

"And we were robbed in front of a room full of people?"

"I wouldn't say quite full...."

"But you get my meaning."

"Sure."

"So then... your company should have no problem covering our policy."

I shrugged. "Honestly, sir, that's claims and claims adjustment. I'm just the guy who makes sure they're completely clear on what happened. Your adjuster will figure out that other stuff once I make my report."

He seemed to accept that and leaned back in his chair, but then added, "Well that's fine; but it doesn't explain your need to come over here and interrogate me. I don't see why you felt the need to take such... to come over here, like I've done something wrong."

Now, consider that I had not yet asked this man a question.

There are certain signs of a guilty conscience that do not

take a great surplus of intuition to spot. When a man starts spluttering about his lack of guilt before any such guilt has even been proposed? That would be one.

I said, "Sir, is there something you need to tell me?" My brother Davy joked sometimes that it was the line he used more in day to day work as policeman than any other… aside from "have we been drinking this evening?"

He leaned back again, playing with a fountain pen, crossing one leg over the other. "Nothing. No, there's nothing."

"Because it's just routine procedure in every large claim to go over pertinent details and meet with everyone involved. Additionally, you were a witness to the theft…"

"Inasmuch as any of us was, Mr. Quinn." He leaned forward and put the pen down on the desk. Then he arched his fingers slightly and lowered his voice, as if speaking to a child. "You see, I didn't see much. I was on the floor at the time, trying to avoid having my head blown off."

"Yes, sir…"

"So I didn't really see anything. Nothing. In fact, I wouldn't be surprised if everyone there gave you basically the same perspective."

"Yes, sir. That's not really what I wanted to ask you about."

He wasn't sure where I was going with it, so he backed down. "Oh."

"Mr. DeGoey, you're in a lot of financial difficulty, a lot of trouble. Did it occur to you that someone might have stolen the painting to damage you personally? Between the insurance hit, the bad press…"

He snorted and leaned back again. "Where did you get that idea?"

"Which, the…"

"The financial difficulty, as you put it. Does it look like

I'm having financial difficulty?" He waved his hand around the room.

He sounded like Dibartolo. I took a pause before answering and tried to look a little exasperated. "Mr. DeGoey, I'm a professional insurance investigator. Your debts aren't particularly hidden. It's public paper, sir."

DeGoey pulled his chair forward and leaned on his desk, pondering what tack to take next. He looked down at a writing pad calendar unhappily. "It's all a bit like a house of cards right now, you know? Like one bad push…"

Realizing that I knew about the red ink had wilted his resolve, and now the businessman just looked tired. "You spend years building up your business, and you get so involved, sometimes you don't see the problems until it's too late."

I point out at this juncture that it's my brother Andy who's the priest. I don't take confessional, and guys living on other people's money, like DeGoey, only ever sought as much support as was required to con the guy across the table or to try and get others to feel sorry for them. My sympathy cup did not exactly runneth over.

"Had anyone inquired about buying the building? There must have been pressure from the banks to sell such a prime piece of real estate."

"By the day. And I'd just as soon get it all over with. If I could sell out and cover my creditors, don't you think I'd do that?"

"So why not?"

DeGoey sighed. One of the reasons gangsters like to get businesses in trouble before they "bail them out" is that it's normal for those businesses to operate within confidentiality clauses. But DeGoey's fatigue suggested he was tired of keeping his mouth shut.

"My partner, Carl Hecht. He has a veto on the sale of

any capital assets that he slipped into our partnership agreement a few years ago; when he extended me some ... help."

"Why would he do that?"

"He's a full partner. As long as the company is still technically solvent, he has the power to draw on credit, and to find more."

"So he's bleeding you dry."

"I didn't say that."

He didn't have to. Hecht's racket was as old as the hills, a favorite of wise guys going back to the days of Angelo Bruno and Phil Testa. It also usually wasn't a hand anyone played without the implied threat of violence to back it up.

First, the gangster advances the business some liquid support, a little cash to tide them over. Then his crew starts working behind the scenes to tear the business down – robberies, arson, graffiti, threatening customers; anything they can do to make the businessman think he needs help from his generous wise guy friend, the guy who advanced him a few bucks. Now, he's paying security to the wise guy.

But after a few weeks, the wise guy expresses misgivings, concern that his friend is taking all the business risk and paying the wise guy for doing nothing. So he offers to go in with him, invest the money needed to REALLY make the business take off.

And that's all it takes. Once the wise guy is a full partner, all bets are off; he'll bleed the place until neither it nor the guarantor of all that credit – the other partner – has anything left.

"What's Hecht's racket. When he's not putting the screws to you?"

"Putting the screws to me? His 'racket'? Are you referring to his main business?"

Are you stalling trying to think of an answer? "As you say, Mr.

DeGoey. What was his main business?"

DeGoey wasn't accustomed to a lot of questions, and he paused for a few seconds and squirmed in his chair while struggling for a tactful response. Finally, he composed himself. "I suppose that's a question you'd have to ask Mr. Hecht. I would simply describe him as a businessman."

"I suppose I will have to talk to him."

He looked nervous. "Is that really necessary? Dennis and Carl are very busy men, after all. I'm not sure they'd enjoy having you bother them."

I studied him for a second or two before replying. He was trying so hard to look calm and collected. "Mr. DeGoey, are you afraid of your partner? Because I get the feeling maybe you should be talking to the police. I know what that sounds like, and people always have this idea from TVs and movies that they'd be better off with their yaps shut. But the reality isn't quite like that.

He didn't reply right away. DeGoey's gaze flitted to the door, then back to me. He crossed his arms. It was obvious he was getting uncomfortable talking abut his sleazy partner. He stood then flourished his arm towards the door. "I won't be keeping you any longer, Mr. Quinn. I presume you have everything you need."

I got up and smiled, heading for the exit.

"Not even close."

13.

Carl Hecht's lawyer of record on court document was John Guglioni and his office was just a few blocks away, so I hoofed it over. The sidewalks south of Center City weren't exactly teeming with pedestrians, and the storefronts had that sad, vacant quality you notice when someone ignored the old maxim of location above all.

The building was another anonymous tower, although Guglioni's firm was high-powered enough to have brought in a designer, so the décor was exceptional, right down to the immaculately framed Matisse prints on the rose-marble back wall. The receptionist was the type who preferred the title "assistant," wore a power suit and yet had no pause in bringing someone a cup of coffee while they waited.

As long as the person waiting wasn't me; she looked up from her computer and shook her head gently. "Mr. Guglioni's going to be very busy today, Mr... "

"Quinn." I gave her my brightest, warmest smile, but I might as well have been flirting with a traffic cone.

"Yeeesss, well Mr. Quinn, I'm sorry but Mr. Guglioni is a very busy man generally, and without an appointment..."

"I've left a few messages here for Mr. Guglioni's client, Carl Hecht. Is there a chance you could ensure he gets my number?"

She didn't even look up this time. "We are glad you stopped by Mr. Quinn, and I'm sorry that I couldn't be more help."

That was about as friendly as I'd expected.

On the way back down to street level in the elevator, I thought about the robbery again. The biggest problem was if no one there that day was involved, or it was unconnected to the local arts community. Something like that would mean relying on criminal contacts, which was always hazardous but especially so to a guy on parole. Art robberies weren't unheard of, after all, and it wasn't always an appreciator pulling the strings; plenty of people were just in it for the money, and the Vermeer had been an easy target.

But I couldn't help that nagging feeling that there was something off about the execution of the whole thing, about the absence of interest in other paintings, or in robbing the patrons, who had who-knows-how-much access to cash and credit.

It was like Dibartolo had noted: there was some sleight-of-hand going on. For one, there was still that other picture they'd messed with -- I was going to need some help with that, as I wasn't familiar with the work. And then there was the question of who the two guys were who stopped by my apartment building.

If all of that wasn't a good enough excuse for missing Ma's Sunday dinner, I didn't know what would be.

Actually, I did: absolutely nothing. Absolutely nothing was a good enough excuse for missing Ma's Sunday dinner.

When it came to the murky motivations of the kind of bad guys I sometimes ran into, on the other hand, it didn't hurt to have spent more than three years in the pen. It gave me a chance to make some decent contacts in the world of serious larceny.

One of those was Danny Saint, a frizzy-haired former pitcher in the Phillies farm system who'd gotten caught trying to smuggle eight pounds of weed into Washington State from Canada during the offseason. We'd actually known each other as young kids then lost touch when he moved.

After a few years inside, he'd become as adept at short cons and grifting as anyone you'd want to meet, and he was usually hanging around a corner somewhere downtown. If not, he was hustling pool at O'Connor's or one of the other two-bit dives that were just close enough to his turf to save the soles of his shoes.

On this occasion, it was a Three Card Monte table just off Washington Square. He was seated at a card table on the sidewalk, a player across from him trying to guess which of three cards, creased horizontally and laid parallel on the table, was the one they'd originally chosen.

Three-Card Monte is a con, but many people to this day think it's a legitimate game, because the operator uses a shill – a confederate in the crowd who "wins" the odd hand. Danny knew enough other local hustlers to get a new one to stop by every few hours in exchange for that hand, so that it looked like different people winning.

The first time some fool in the crowd put up more than a ten spot, Danny would palm away the real hole card and replace it, so that the player had no chance of winning. The only way to know the card was no longer in play would be to flip the other two, which no decent operator would let happen.

Palming involves bending the card just slightly enough to grip it in the palm when all of the operator's fingers are together, which is why Three-Card Monte cards are usually generously creased. Danny learned his technique from *Blackstone's Card Tricks and Secrets of Magic*, an old textbook on the arts by the greatest magician of the early part of the century, Harry Blackstone. Danny was also a hell of a crooked dealer, another one we could blame on old Harry.

Judging by the speed of his hands and the big smile on his face, he was having a good day, a steady patter keeping the half-dozen onlookers entertained, taking a moment out of their shopping to feel a little dangerous.

"Yes! We have a winner!" he said, handing ten dollars over to a big black guy in a pale blue round-neck windbreaker. The man held up the bill ceremoniously then kissed it, getting a couple of happy claps from the other onlookers.

I'd seen him somewhere before but couldn't place it...

TV. I'd seen him in a local mattress commercial. I wasn't allowed to paint when I got out of the can as a part of my conditions and I'm not ashamed to admit I got a little addicted to afternoon soaps.

Once Danny saw me, he realized something was up. "Okay, folks, I know when I'm beat. I've lost enough money today, so I'm going to pack it up now for lunch. Always here, always around, always the best card game in town."

The crowd dispersed. He started packing his game up. "I had to move soon anyway. But could you have waited until I wasn't working Liam? Geez."

"Sorry, Danny. It's kind of a big case, which always means working against the clock."

"What do you need?" Danny owed me many, many favors from inside the joint, not the least of which was protecting his delicate virtue from the gangs.

"There was a gallery knocked over a few days ago, along Chestnut."

"Yeah. Yeah, I heard about that. They got some fancy painting or something."

"Something like that, yeah. Listen," I said, talking low. "I need you to put the word out, see what you can find out about it. Aside from the fancy one, the Vermeer, they may have stolen another one, a more modern painting, and replaced it with a fake. I don't know about that bit for sure yet, but it's worth asking."

"Okay, you got it man. Hey... you want to help me get my game going again? I could use a new shill if you're looking for lunch money."

I shook my head. "We're both on parole, Danny. I'm not

even supposed to talk to you, remember?"

I'll never quite understand why Danny didn't have as acute a sense of either morality or the fear of getting caught as most folks. But that stuff didn't faze him at all. "Poor impulse control," is what the prison shrinks called it. They blamed it on the fact that he didn't get much attention as a kid, which made him feel insecure, and on his ADHD, a learning disability that affects the emotional maturity end more than intelligence.

He beat the odds and almost made the big leagues in two ways: by impressing people with his fastball and with his good nature.

He didn't have the fastball anymore, or the baseball career. So he had to rely on the good nature. Of course, while he was good naturedly telling you a joke, he was also good naturedly removing your wallet from your back pocket.

"And yet here you are," he said, nodding knowingly. He riffled though the deck. "Are you sure you don't want in, Liam? This beats the hell out of working for a living."

"Or trying to throw a breaking ball?"

He laughed. "Yeah, especially that." In Danny's one spring training call up, the big leaguers had teed off on his curve ball like it wasn't even moving. He'd joked that so many of his breaking balls went over the fence, they saw more of Florida than he did.

I smiled, but said no. "Besides, you seem to have enough friends helping you out already. Didn't I see that guy in a mattress commercial?"

The young grifter nodded, smiling with his tongue sticking out a little, absolutely pleased with himself. "My latest idea: there are thousands of out-of-work actors who don't mind stopping by for a quick ten spot. They get some practice and a free lunch, and I get a much broader cast."

"And the guilt… it doesn't get to you, cheating them?" I

don't know why I asked him the hard question, the one crooks hate talking about.

He sniffed at that and flushed, slightly embarrassed. "Ahhh... don't kid yourself! They know it's a con. They're just sure they can catch me out, is all. It's greed, but it's their choice."

"Don't you worry about someone turning you in, what with extra people involved? The more who know, right?"

"Nah," he waved a hand absentmindedly. "Division of labor."

"You're a regular Henry Ford, Danny."

He looked puzzled. "The guy from Raiders? Han Solo?"

I nodded. "Yeah. That's what I meant. You're like Han Solo."

He liked that, trying to squint coolly, like a bad guy – which Danny just wasn't, no matter how hard he tried. "Bitchin'," he said.

Han Solo couldn't have put it better himself.

14.

The issue of the second painting, on the other hand, was going to take someone a lot smoother than Danny and a lot more legitimate. What I knew about it so far didn't seem to make any sense, and Danny was never big on contributing sense to a discussion.

But my best friend was chock-full of the stuff. If you added smart, passionate, funny and beautiful to the mix, you pretty much had Nora Garcia de Soria.

She'd sounded eager to meet me at the DeGoey Gallery, as we hadn't talked in some time.

I met Nora in junior high school, and fell in love with her on first sight.

Most guys did.

Her coppery-auburn-red hair cascaded down in light ringlets, and her skin was as smooth as a laconic clarinet solo, cocoa brown under burning green eyes. A lithe five-foot eight inches, narrow-waisted and broad hipped, she walked with poise and purpose. When she sashayed into a room, the women stopped talking and the men began mentally reassessing their life choices.

We'd been "buddies" since the eighth grade. And yeah, that's as agonizing sometimes as it sounds. I try to be mature about it and not jealous of... any guy she dates, pretty much. I do a good job of hiding it, and a lousy job of not really giving a damn. If you met her, you'd understand.

On the upside, my going to jail hadn't even slowed her down. She'd visited regularly; in fact, we talked more often back then, when she had to come to Curran-Fromhold to see me, than we did now. She had a sweet condo on the fifteenth floor of a highrise, downtown, ten minutes from my folks' place.

When I first got out, we were tight. We had lunch every day, hung out on weekends, talked about our future plans. We might as well have been back in high school.

That had continued until a few months ago. I hadn't told her but reassessing my life had included reconsidering our friendship. I just loved her too damn much; she wasn't ever going to see it and I wasn't going to feel worthy enough to tell her. And, at that point, it's just inconsiderate obsession.

But I was as conflicted as Hell; love and passion were one side of the equation, but she really was my best friend as well.

I was starting to think it would just be easier to move on – although if I'm honest about it, I hadn't had a girlfriend since getting out of the stir, and the loneliness might have been setting in. I felt possessive, protective – and increasingly beneath her.

Outside the gallery's front doors, she was dressed stylishly in suit pants and a waist-tied short woolen coat. "Liam!" She hugged me. Then she punched me in the shoulder. "Where have you been? We're supposed to be besties and I haven't talked to you in six weeks."

"Yeah ... I had this case. Real nasty piece of work, a big biker…"

"You said you were going to be working on something."

"He was pretending to be dead. Words were briefly exchanged. Things got a little heated."

"Heated?"

"Inflated."

"Inflated?"

"Conflicted. You know. Hey, he tried to hit me with a pool cue, okay? He said some things, I said some things back…"

She rolled her eyes.

"What?"

"You're so talented. Why aren't you creating, painting, instead of brawling with lowlifes? I mean, it's not like you're ever going to learn not to be a smart-ass, not at this point. But you can work around that..."

I looked sideways, momentarily embarrassed. "I have to pay the bills like anyone else."

"You know, I still have that drawing you did of me in high school."

I'd sketched her when she'd fallen asleep in chemistry class, using her crooked arm as a pillow and resting her head on her desk. She'd hardly changed, as far as I could tell.

"Long time ago. We were kids."

She shrugged. "Not so long. I don't feel old. You?"

I smiled. "Not so much. Older than before the pen."

"You still need to get a real job. You deserve better than weekends at dive bars or chasing arsonists."

She believed that a lot more than I did. I'd see the toll my decisions had taken on loved ones. Most weren't as forgiving or unaffected as she'd behaved. "I didn't have that many options when I got out. Probably wouldn't have been doing this without help from your dad. I mean... I wouldn't. Without his recommendation, I don't get a provisional license."

"I guess being a cop was out of the question," she said with a little giggle. You couldn't be friends with Nora without taking a regular ribbing.

I gave her a venomous squint. "All right, all right, you've had your fun picking on me for the day. Let me show you this painting." I pulled opent he glass-fronted door to the gallery.

Inside, Stephanie was preoccupied, and the other staff were hiding somewhere in the back. Alison Pace was nowhere to be seen. So we strolled along, studying the walls.

Nora said, "I guess I'll have to say hi to her some other time."

The painting was modern abstract, infused with an almost naïve stroke, like a child expressing nonsense but producing evocative imagery nonetheless, splashes of color that reminded the onlooker of a day outside. It was optimistic and still open enough to individual definition to qualify as abstract, rather than impressionist.

Nora smiled as soon as she saw it. "It's a Dufresne. He's a local artist who's gathered a large following in the last few years. This is an early piece called "Autumn Mist" – I saw it last year at a private showing. It's just... I think it's neat. Right? I mean, it makes you think about so many different things."

"Dufresne himself was here on the afternoon of the robbery," I said. "Alison said he'd been trying to get more wall space. Look, do me a favor and take a really close look at the brushwork. I think it might be a really good copy."

"Sure." She got in close, check out the texture of the strokes in the oil paint, examining the whorls from different angles, then peering at the signature. Then she pulled a small jeweler's loop out of her pocket and took an even closer look.

15.

It's not the easiest job, detecting a modern art fake.

Unlike older works, which are often detected purely by using poor aging techniques or inappropriately dated tools, an authenticator looking at a modern piece has to rely almost exclusively on the artist's personal technique: the amount of paint left in each whorl at the end of a brush stroke; the angles and perspectives used, the amount of paint used in the stroke, the blend of colors and shades.

"Well?"

Nora pulled away from the loop. "Even with the lighting being less than optimal, I can tell you absolutely, positively one hundred percent guaranteed, it's the genuine article."

That blew my first theory. Why would the robber take it off the wall, inspect it, and put it back? I'd felt certain he'd switched the painting out. "You're that sure?"

She punched me in the shoulder again. Only, instead of an actual punch she used an abrupt, withering glance to the exact same effect.

"Ouch! Okay, okay, stupid question."

"Besides, don't you think Dufresne would have spotted a forgery of his own work? And why would they leave a copy of one stolen painting behind, but not the other?"

Fair points. I had no answers yet.

"It could be anything. Maybe they only had time for one. Maybe they couldn't get someone good enough to handle the Vermeer. There are plenty of artists who don't pay close enough attention to the small details. Any decent forger knows that."

Then I realized what I'd said, and we both stood there, awkwardly silent in the moment.

"Sorry."

"I know what you meant. It's all good."

"I'm sorry I ever even put you in that position. I'm an idiot." It's true. It doesn't matter how gifted or smart a person is in one or even a few areas of their life; it doesn't prevent them from being idiots in almost every other respect. I'd made an art form out of it in recent years.

"You were young and stupid, and the money was even stupider. I might have been dumb enough, too…"

I interjected. "No. You'd have never done something that crazy and wrong." I never tried to sugar-coat it for her. I'd met some bad guys and made bad, selfish decisions. There was no atonement for that, no turning back the clock. You can never undo a wrong; you can only try to do right from there on. You can never assume people will forget, you can only hope you earn their forgiveness. But giving it is up to them, the ones wronged, not you, the one who wronged them.

And by 'you', I mean 'me.' There's that guilt kicking in again.

She turned her head and looked deeply into my eyes from just a few inches away. There was a softness in her gaze, even close and direct.

"Don't think you know everything about me, Liam Quinn. Everybody has their secrets … the things they'd may be like to tell someone else, but just can't. We've all got them, and although you sometimes act like it, I'm not perfect. In fact, it would take some pressure off sometimes if you'd realize I'm not perfect. None of us are. Right?"

Didn't I know it! I dropped my head reflexively, feeling ashamed.

"So…" She took a deep breath, breaking the tension, "…how does this help you with the robbery investigation, exactly?"

"I wish I knew. Listen," I asked, "you doing anything tomorrow afternoon?"

She thought about it. "I was going to work on the basement." Nora had been renovating an old house just off the downtown core, a beautiful old A-frame with a lot that would've accommodated two entire walk-ups in Fishtown; she was intending to sell it for a quick profit or rent it to college students.

"I have to check out the soccer game at PPL Park in Chester. It's work, technically, but they gave me great seats and it's a great time."

She looked skeptical. "Soccer?" Nora didn't care about any sport except the Eagles, ever since Randall Cunningham signed a ball cap for her as a kid. The Birds occupied a fair chunk of Sundays in Nora's year, and she could flap those arms and squawk with the loudest of bare-chested, drunken fanboys.

"I promise, you'll love it. This isn't like high school soccer, these guys play with grace, style, technique…"

She was smiling oddly. I said, "What?" I thought I had food on my face or something.

But Nora just shook her head. "European boys in short shorts. Yum! Plus, I just love seeing you happy. It's a good thing to see. Different."

And I couldn't help but smile at that myself.

We went our separate ways outside the gallery, and I took a look back as she made her way down the sidewalk in the opposite direction. She took a quick glance back as well, and I figured that, if nothing else, it felt sort of good to know she was still thinking of me.

I'd parked a couple of blocks away. I walked back to the car and was just unlocking the driver's-side door when a couple of heavy guys – in form and temperament – climbed out of the green sedan across the road. One got out of the front passenger seat and the other the back, both wearing the same tan trench coats Ricky had described.

They both headed right towards me, and I contemplated jumping back in the beast and hitting the gas — assuming she'd start — until one of the two pushed his hand up in his pocket, as if concealing a gun.

"We need to talk," said the shorter one. The other guy used the concealed gun to motion us towards the narrow alley nearby.

16.

Ten feet down the alley, the larger one moved to take the gun out of his pocket. Figuring he couldn't pull the trigger with it halfway out, I took the advantage, pivoting quickly and hammering him with a quick roundhouse right shot to the jaw.

There are generally two ways to take a guy down in the ring: you can nail him hard square on the chin, or you can slowly knock the wind out of him by hammering the body, until his legs are gone.

He went down, groggy but not out.

The second, smaller man squared up with me, hands up in a protective stance. Philly is a boxing town, with a huge history, guys like Joe Frazier, Joey Girardello and Miracle Matthew Saad Muhammad, the all-action light heavyweight who shocked the boxing world in the late seventies before joining the nation of Islam. If you ran into a guy with a pug ear or crooked nose and he wanted to fight outside a bar, it was generally always a good idea to assume he might know how throw a punch and back off.

Of course, a great deal many ex-fighters thought they had a lot more talent and natural ability than was the case. Anyone who actually made it – or even came close – instantly knew the difference, just from how they held themselves.

"You made a mistake with that one, sonny," said the squat little thug.

"You figure?" He had his back to the alley now, and we stopped circling.

"Yeah. I was Golden Gloves," he said. "You're about to be taught a lesson, ya dirty mick sonuvabitch."

I smirked. "Golden Gloves? You? In... what, Fifty-two? When you got back from Korea?"

"Pretty funny. Won't be laughing after I wipe the floor with you."

"The only thing you wiped up any time recent was extra helpings of gravy, ya fat bastard."

He threw a crisp jab, but he was slow and his reach was poor. I feinted left and watched it go by like a slow-motion intrusion.

"That the best you got?" I dropped my right shoulder a little so he'd think the big punch was coming, and instead flicked a couple of sharp left-hand jabs out. The first hit him flush in the nose, which started to bleed. The second one gave him a fat lip. He half-stepped backwards and shook his head, momentarily stunned.

"That... the best..."

"Nope," I said, hitting him with a roundhouse body shot that knocked his wind out. He started to double over, and as his chin dropped slightly I threw a left cross that caught him on the button, knocking him out, face down in the wet gravel and dirt of the alley.

The other one was struggling to get up and before he could get the gun out of his pocket, I gave him a swift kick to the temple, putting him down hard.

Then it occurred to me: *if neither of them got out of the driver's side, who was driving the....*

And that was when the blackjack came down, a shuddering rabbit punch from an inch-thick rubber pipe to the back of my head that rattled my teeth. I dropped to my knees.

A voice behind me said, "Not so fast now, are you?" And then the blackjack came down again, and the lights went out.

17.

When you're knocked cold, it's just like being asleep, except instant. One second you're conscious, usually bleating some mouthy jawn to the dude who's about connect before you can duck him.

The next, you're dreaming, usually of something that makes no sense, a jumble of disconnected-yet-real passages, of stumbling through corridors, and fistfights and mournful speeches by lost loves, of splashes of color, yellows and greys and reds, and then of something passionate, green-and-white, red-and-black.

There are glimpses of reality there, too, decisions you made and now regret, the indifference of others who should care. Choices you'd like to take back, but instead just recall and dream about over and over again…

And when you finally wake, it's not for some prosaic reason, like trying to avoid death in a dream so you don't die in real life, or trying to avoid falling, so that you won't have a heart attack from fright before you hit the ground, or anything like that.

It's because a homeless guy who lives in the alley in which you're lying is rifling through your pockets.

That's how it was for me, anyhow.

The feeling of the guy's hands in my pants shocked me awake. My head was pounding from the attack and bruised ribs suggested someone had given me a good kick, probably several.

But I seemed okay otherwise, and when he realized I was coming around, the homeless guy scurried down the alley. The wise guys had split and I had no doubt that if I hadn't taken out the first two, they'd have probably stuck around to finish me off.

It didn't seem likely that the two guys from the gallery heist were trying to keep me from getting involved. They'd be laying low, no matter what they were really up to. But that meant other muscle was involved, and at least three guys at that. They could've been Ricky's heavy visitors, or new players.

And it all added up to much more than just a quick robbery. Why would a crook come into a gallery, take down a painting, then remount it on the wall? Why would he steal from a gallery whose partner is some kind of mobster? That seemed suicidal.

What was the bigger robber up to? Was he trying to find something? Maybe it was the wrong picture. Maybe they were expecting something else in that spot? Or behind it?"

I'd asked Nora that earlier in the day.

"Maybe he grabbed it to steal it then changed his mind, like he realized he had to follow orders or something."

"Doesn't make sense. There was a Beechey there worth at least $60,000. What do you figure that Dufresne would rise to at auction?"

"Maybe…$2,500?"

"So why would a robber even think about taking the picture worth $2,500 when there's another picture worth about twenty five times within darting distance of the front door?"

Like I said, Nora's smart. But she's not psychic. After a second she exhaled deeply. "You got me, Liam."

Yeah. I wish.

The morning before the soccer game, my phone rang early.

My youngest brother, Davy, was working the red-eye shift. That he was calling me at 6:20 a.m. was less surprising than the fact that he was calling at all.

"Listen, I don't really want to talk to you or nothing," he said before I could even acknowledge it was me, "but Pa said if I heard anything you could use I should let you know. So I'm calling because he told me I should."

That's 'Officer David Quinn' to me, apparently.

"So say what you've got to say," I suggested. Like I mentioned, things were tense between us. He was about as warm as a popsicle.

"Fine, I will."

"Okay then. No one's stopping you."

"Dick," he muttered.

"Excuse me?"

"I said you should talk to a robbery dick named Esterhaus, works out of Center City."

"Oh. That's what you said, is it?"

"Yeah. You got a problem with that?"

"No. You know him?"

"Not a bit. If he's smart, he won't talk to your convict ass."

"Yeah... like you'd recognize smart."

"From the dumbest genius anyone ever met to God's ears. He can paint like Picasso, box like Hagler... but he lives in Philly and yet is too stupid to get glass coverage for his car."

"See, when you lecture me, it reminds me you care. It's knowing you care that counts the most."

"Yeah, well... you ain't even close to being done apologizing, far as I'm concerned. If it wasn't going to break Ma's heart, I wouldn't even have a brother."

"You mean other than the priest and the civil servant, right?"

And that was that. Davy hung up on me without another word.

Every time we went a few rounds like that, I felt the weight of how betrayed he felt, of how much I'd let him down.

I went back to work, looking up the number for Esterhaus's precinct house. Davy's anger towards me was still raw and would take longer to heal, him being a serving member and all. Plus, maybe, I still needed to figure out the right things to say. Whatever words would help make it right.

I got Esterhaus's voice mail, leaving my name and a suitably cryptic message about the robbery. That pretty much guaranteed he'd call me back, just to make sure I didn't have info he could use. Then I grabbed a quarter of grapefruit from the refrigerator and some milk, setting both on the small Formica table for breakfast.

After breakfast, I hit the pavement in the neighborhood for a jog, the early morning cool enough and the streets quiet enough to give me a chance to stretch without looking over my shoulder.

When I got back, I hit the speed bag for twenty minutes, angry at myself.

Eventually, he called back. "Well, well, well. The son of the Mighty Quinn," he said. "As I live and breathe."

That was a stumper "Pardon?"

"I knew your father, back in the day when he was busting heads and taking down the bad guys. We worked together a bit, partnered for a while."

That was a surprise. Pa was never shy about talking about his cronies from the force. I figured he'd have mentioned him. "Yeah? Must've been a while ago."

"He didn't mention me?" He sounded bemused. "Not a total shock. But you would have been a little kid anyhow. You wouldn't remember."

I made a mental note to ask my father what was up. "So you're handling the gallery heist?"

"Yeah, such as it is." He didn't sound very enthusiastic. "One painting in a city this big? We'll probably end out shelving this one, letting insurance handle it."

"Yeah, about that...." I filled him in on my job and how much the Vermeer was worth.

He laughed. "I don't envy you, kid. We've been rounding up the usual suspects."

"So... you don't think anyone at the show..."

"Come on!" he said, bemused. "This isn't CSI, kid. In the real world, the crooks don't do you the favor of hanging around and the people who pay them don't come along for the ride to the crime scene. Believe me, this'll be a regular guy from the neighborhood. Maybe we get him, maybe we don't."

"You almost sound like you don't care if you get him at all."

"I've been a cop a long time. Sometimes the breaks don't go our way. You got to learn to let these things slide. You know, your old man would understand."

What the hell was that supposed to mean? "Maybe I'll ask him," I said.

"You do that, kid. Little Liam Quinn... as I live and breathe. Who would've thought of one of Al Quinn's boys growing up? Listen, I've got to run. It's been good catching up though. You know where I am if you need me."

"Yeah, sure. Listen..."

But he'd already hung up.

18.

The crowd was already in full voice by the time we got to the stadium.

If you've never heard a few thousand mildly drunken fans sing in unison, it's a joyous and wonderful thing — particularly if you, also, are mildly drunk.

Participation is not mandatory but is accepted with enthusiastic abandon.

And Nora was enthusiastic. You need to understand: this is one straight-laced woman. She never drinks much more than coffee, and only has the odd glass of champagne at the usual dozen weddings she has to attend every summer.

But sports venues were another matter, like a refuge for the wild at heart, an uncaged chorus of tribalism. And lately for some reason, she seemed to want to cut loose a bit. We'd stopped for lunch before heading down to Chester and she'd finished off a small carafe of white wine. Then we each got a pint of beer when they opened the gates.

By the time we made our way to our seats, about three rows up from the players' benches, she was joining in without hesitation. She belted the fight song; she took part in the 'wave'; and when the Union scored off a corner, the tall defender nodding the ball into the far side of the net, she jumped to her feet so quickly she almost fell over, and I had to catch her.

We settled back into our seats, with Nora on pint number two. I was working – although it didn't feel much like it – so one was my limit, and I'd be lying if I said I wasn't a little jealous. It was a cool, breezy afternoon by the river, and she gripped my elbow both to get warm and to release the tension of the game.

I watched her quietly for a minute in profile, her green eyes flicking back and forth as she followed the play. The Union were in good form, passing circles around Toronto, and it was obvious she'd been caught in the spell.

She had an almost innocent quality, an innate goodness to her. It wasn't hard to love her, and it wasn't hard to feel unworthy.

"Why haven't I done this before?" she asked. Then she quarter-turned and punched me in the shoulder. "Why didn't you tell me how fun this was?"

"I've been trying to get you to come to a game all season."

"Well...yeah. But you didn't tell me it was such a blast."

The half-dozen hardcore fans right behind us started singing one of the player's names to the tune of "La Cucaracha", and Nora joined in for a few seconds.

"I think I'm getting a little drunk," she said, once she'd sat down again.

"You keep putting them back at this rate and I'll have to carry you out of here."

"Ooh," she said mockingly. "Is the big, strong man going to take care of little ol' me?"

"The big, strong man is going to be left with no choice in short order."

She laughed. "Don't worry, spoilsport, I'll slow it down."

Story of our relationship. "Listen, at halftime, I have to head down to the concessions to talk to a couple of the young guys down there. Work stuff."

Nora rolled her eyes. "Yeah, you're a bunch of fun."

"The tickets were free, remember?"

She looked at the foam in the bottom of her empty plastic beer cup. "Wish the beverages were free," she said. "Can you... "

"Drunky. Sure, I'll stop on the way back, okay?"

I filed my way through the crowds on the cement concourse. The vendor was at the far end, towards one of the sets of washrooms, a fake wood counter and three kids in paper hats.

"Welcome to McFinnigan's, what can I get you?" the kid at the counter asked.

Now, as a good Irish-American laddie, I feel compelled to point out that "McFinnigan" is not an Irish name. It's made up to sound like one, just as no one at your average Outback Steakhouse has ever trekked through the Australian desert hunting kangaroo.

The security boss, Bryson, had given me a rundown on the three kids who'd been working that night. DeShawn Ellis was the kid behind the register. That made the short, tubby kid manning the ice cream station the assistant manager, Jeffrey Tillis, and the tall brunette kid near the back David Mince.

"Someone opened the doors to the loading dock so that they could back a pickup in," Bryson had told me. "If our guys are involved and you can get one of them to rollover on the other two, we might have something."

I asked the kid for two beers and waited until he'd started pouring and was a captive audience. "Hey, isn't McFinnigans the franchise that got robbed, like, ten days ago?"

He looked up quickly but avoided eye contact "Yeah."

"Scary, man. Were you here?"

"No."

"Not working that day, huh?" The tubby assistant manager had begun to pay attention.

He brought the two beers to the counter. "That'll be twelve dollars."

"So you weren't working?"

"Yeah... no. I mean, it was after hours." Out of the

corner of my eye I watched the assistant manager shoot a sharp look at the brunette kid near the back.

"Must have made you think twice about coming back, eh?"

DeShawn looked nervous and chewed his lower lip slightly. "Yeah, sure. Look, I have to help the next customer."

"Sure, sure, sorry. Let me get out of your way here..." I moved the two beer glasses onto the adjacent counter, above the ice cream tubs. The assistant manager, Jeffrey, studied me anxiously, waiting me to ask something. He had a burn mark on the inside of his forearm, like from a cigarette, and I pointed to it.

"How'd you do that?"

"Leaned on the stove at home," he lied. The shape was unmistakable.

"Really? 'Cause I just got out of the joint after three years, and I saw a lot of cigarette burns inside. And that looks a hell of a lot like a cigarette burn to me." I said it loud enough for the kid in the back to hear it.

He drew his arm away subconsciously and covered the burn mark with his other hand. "It's nothing."

The skinny brunette kid was listening as intently as possible without it being obvious.

"Hey," I told the other kid. "My mistake. What do I know, right? Cheers."

I left my card on the counter and the kid looking puzzled, which was good. Then I caught up with Nora for the remainder of the game. The Union held out for a win, she had a great time — spending more time standing than sitting, always a sign of a good game — and all was right with the world.

When we got back downtown, I drove Nora over to her parents' place, where she was meeting the rest of her family for dinner.

The Garcia de Sorias lived in Fishtown, too, but it's a big neighborhood. They'd come up in the world in the fifteen years after Ramon took "early retirement" from the force, a euphemism for a reduced pension. He'd signed up at nineteen, so he still had plenty of time after his police career to put his security knowledge to good use.

PMI paid him a ton of dough, I'm sure. I wasn't going up this time, but I'd seen their condo plenty of times and it was stunning: marble floors and kitchen counters, ultra-modern pulls on the cabinets, lean modernist furniture. There was no doubting that man had taste — or at the very least had married it. I wasn't sure who gave Nora the gift, but I had to suspect it was her mother, Brenda.

I let her off outside the building's front doors. I like Ramon, but it was Saturday, and when I was away from the office the idea of not talking to the boss had a certain appeal.

"Not coming up? My mom will be crushed. She loves you, you know."

Nora's mom should've been a national treasure. She raised four really great kids on a cop's salary, and I don't think a minute ever went by that she wasn't smiling warmly.

She had large, fluffy blonde "mom" hair but was all of four-feet-eleven inches tall, which gave her a kind of magical quality, especially when she'd just baked one of her pies. Kids loved her even more than adults, like a magic elf or a particularly cheerful fairy godmother.

"Nah. I have to get back to work," I lied.

Truth was, hanging out with Nora was that double-edged sword that cut both ways: chances are neither of us would be happier any time that week ... but she was still going out on a date the next Monday with some schnook from the museum.

Like I said, when it came to women like Nora, I was out of my league.

19.

Halfway back to my place my phone rang. I pulled over and answered; I'm a great believer that, despite the world's insistence on carrying a phone everywhere, few calls were ever worth dying for.

"Is this Quinn?"

"Depends."

"That's a yes."

"That's an 'I have an off button'."

"Carl Hecht. You wanted to talk to me?"

"I still do."

"So shoot."

"I'm investigating ..."

"I know why you were calling. Get on with it."

Direct. Well, it was going to save time.

"Mr. Hecht, did you arrange to have that gallery robbed?"

"Huh. Now why would I do that?"

"Word is you're a silent partner and things aren't going well."

"So?"

"So maybe DeGoey is forced to sell and you structure it to get a cut before his creditors, for one."

He chuckled. "That's pretty creative."

"Thank you."

"Not smart, though. If I was going to pay someone to rob the place, why would I do it on the one day of the week that I'm visiting?"

"Because if you weren't there, you might have been the first person DeGoey suspected."

He chuckled again. "So if I'm there, I'm a suspect because I'm there. But if I'm not there, I'm a suspect because

I'm not there? How's that one supposed to work on my favor?"

"Okay, that's a decent point. But... it's also why we're talking. I have to covert the basis. And... he does seem scared of you."

"I think you're overrating how much I worry about John's feelings."

"Duly noted."

"I'm not some hoodlum, Mr. Quinn, I'm a businessman. That can be messy enough."

It should also be noted that when a guy says "I'm not some hoodlum," it usually means he is, in fact, quite the hoodlum.

"Oh yeah?"

"Listen, I'll keep it short and simple, Mr. Quinn. I like being in business with John. It's unfortunate that he has run into some trouble financially, but that's business sometimes. I try to help where I can, but I have my own concerns. But I don't know anything about that robbery — other than how shocking it was to go through it, of course."

"Of course."

"Good talking to you."

Click.

And that was all I was going to get from Hecht. I hung up the phone and put it back in my pocket, but before I could even pull the car back out into traffic, it rang again.

"Liam? Walter Beck."

"Been awhile, Walter."

"Indeed, my boy, indeed. Would you have time to grab a spot of lunch tomorrow?

"I guess. What's the subject?"

He sounded giddy. "I hear you're working on quite a case, my boy. I'm thinking we need to go over the pertinent details."

"You've been talking to Leo Tesser." Like a dutiful student, Alison's boyfriend had probably gone right back to his boss.

"He's a nice boy, but he doesn't necessarily see the potential in these things."

Walter had always been a showman. He got most of his clients acquitted, but he also got the pick of the best clients by knowing how to capitalize on something public.

The gallery robbery wasn't a big story, as long it stayed just that: a straight snatch-and-run by a couple of thugs. But Walter was smart enough to know that if something else came up in the insurance investigation, suddenly the story might have public relations legs.

"Got a favorite spot?" I asked

"How about Modo Mio? Italian joint off ..."

"Are you kidding? It's a few blocks from my parents' house. Good food."

We arranged to meet at 1 p.m.

"Looking forward to it, my boy," he said.

Any time Walter was that happy, it had to be bad news for somebody.

I went back home and worked on my foot movement, dancing circles around the heavy bag, making sure to keep them wide enough to be balanced, but narrow enough to be mobile, staying on my toes.

It's not that I ever expected to compete in the ring again; there's just something relaxing about the consistency of the exercise, taking half steps then shuffling a few paces sideways, stepping up, shuffling back, then bob and weave, then throw, then shuffle out. If I hadn't gotten back into boxing in prison, I might have gone stir crazy, as its library wasn't exactly extensive.

Nora had called earlier in the day and left a message on my land line but I didn't return it until after my workout. I got changed into boxers and an undershirt, brewed some tea and put my feet up in front of the TV, turning it on with the sounded muted before I dialed her back.

"Hey you," she said. "You're finally home."

"Working man."

"Even weekends?"

"Especially weekends."

She chortled. "I really enjoyed the game today. Awesome."

"Yeah, nothing like free tickets."

"And cold beer."

"And a good game."

"And the company was nice, too."

I said, "Yeah, wasn't the crowd something else today? Wow."

She sighed. "I was thinking more that it was a nice place to take someone special."

"Yeah? So what, you're going to take a date the next time you go and leave me behind?"

Nora was silent for a few seconds. "Sometimes I wonder if you were hit in the head too many times when you were a fighter, you know that?"

"Very funny. Hey, everybody, it's Nora, the standup from Fishtown."

She said, "So what are you doing for the rest of the night?"

"Nothing. Just worked out. Going to watch a little T.V. Then I'll probably hit the sack."

"Mr. Excitement."

"It's hardly the heady thrill of being an art curator...but hey, you know me."

She laughed. "I'm glad I do, at that. Why aren't you

working on any of your art?" She knew my probationary restriction had already passed, but I still wasn't interested. So I changed the subject.

"Are you going to come with me to next week's game? They're home again, to D.C."

"Ahhh… damn. I can't. My cousin Ellie is getting married and I'm in the wedding party."

"You'd skip the Union and an afternoon with yours truly for a horrendous bridesmaid's dress? Couldn't you tell them you have a flesh-eating disease, or something?"

She laughed. "I don't think they'd buy it. I'd have to amputate a leg before I could go back to work."

"And then you couldn't go to soccer with me no more, what with the jealousy, watching those guys run around all afternoon, and you with your one good leg."

We both chuckled. It was an entirely stupid conversation, which is what we usually enjoyed most. But I was tired, and I'd run out of things to say. I wanted her to keep talking. I always wanted Nora to keep talking.

Instead, she just sighed again and said, "Goodnight, Liam."

"Goodnight Nora."

The small corner restaurant had windows smudged as much by age as dust, and the door creaked on its spring when we entered. Inside, booths lined both walls, and a simple cash register upfront lowered the pretension level.

It was busy for a Sunday, and the only table was at the back near the washrooms.

"Way to reserve us a decent spot, Walter," I said sarcastically as I joined him, reaching across the red-and-white checked tablecloth to shake his hand.

"You have to try the Agnolotti, my boy. It's a wonderful homemade ravioli that they prepare with a mixture of rabbit and veal. Absolutely delicious."

I laughed. "I've had just about everything on the menu. You want something amazing? Try the Razze. It's fresh skate in marsala, almond and asparagus butter. My neighbor Mrs. Pescatelli makes it, and even hers isn't as good as this place."

Walter looked up to the Heavens and mouthed a silent prayer of thank you. "I love good food, my boy. There's nothing like a neighborhood joint where the chef is just cooking home dishes from the old country."

"I didn't know you were religious, Walter."

He shrugged. "I find we all need some help from the man upstairs sometimes, so it helps to stay in touch."

Seemed futile to me; Walter's various and sundry sins would cost more to bail out than any church had on offer. That was before you factored in any moral responsibility for keeping so many lowlifes on the street.

We ordered a bottle of wine, along with some polpo and bruschetta for appetizers. Once the waiter had taken our order, Walter leaned in. "All right, my boy, spill it: what's the story with the gallery robbery?"

"You got me."

"Really?"

"Really. It's a robbery. So far, that's all I really know."

"But you've been asking a lot of questions nonetheless, all over town. I understand the Hecht brothers, among others are less than happy with you."

"You know them?"

"I know of them – in a 'I know of several rationales to stay the hell away from them' sort of way. The word is they've got some very organized friends, if you get my drift. You need to keep your head down."

"I'm trying."

"Really? It sounds like you're spinning around in circles."

"Well sure. But that sort of makes sense when you don't know much about a situation, right?" He was probably right but I wasn't going to admit it.

He thought about it for a moment as the waiter set down our appetizers. "Okay, I'll give you your due. What makes you think there's an inside connection? Why not just random guys?"

I shook my head. "Doesn't sit right. The Vermeer was the only piece they touched, despite some old other works. That's someone with some knowledge." I didn't mention the Dufresne; my instincts told me keeping back the quirkier aspects might keep Walter off my back later on.

"Sure; but why someone there that day? Why attend one's own robbery?"

"For the simple reason that right now the only half-dozen people the Philly cops aren't particularly interested in are the people who were there at the time. They figure it the same way as you."

His eyes narrowed. "But you figure it different."

I nodded. "I haven't figured anything yet, Walter, but there's definitely something going on. Your student, Leo Tesser…"

"Now, Liam, my boy, be nice…"

"No, I'm not suggesting he's involved. But he was there…"

"And he seemed shaken senseless by it. To be frank, he was so frightened by it that I worried about his constitution, whether he had the mettle to be a criminal defense attorney."

That seemed harsh. "You have to admit: he was facing down a pair of shotguns, Walter…"

"Oh, pish! There are people he'll have to deal with in the system – clients, cops… judges – that make the risk of being shot seem like a weekend at Club Med."

"No signs of him spending any new dough, or mentioning getting out of town for a while? Anything that might suggest he made a buck off the proceedings?"

He shook his head. "No, not at all. But now that you mention it, the firm could use his first-hand expertise in our defense of whoever those two poor, disillusioned and disadvantaged individuals were. I mean... they're going to need solid legal representation, after all. Right, my boy?"

Walter's morals were so flexible they could do the splits. "Walter...have you ever considered before you took on a client whether they actually committed the crime?"

His eyes twinkled. "The system only works if everyone gets a good defence, Liam. Guilty, not guilty... that's not my business. In fact, I make it clear that I don't really want to hear it either way."

"As long as they don't move in next door to you when they get out?"

He leaned across the table conspiratorially and whispered under the lunch time din. "I'm on the twenty-third floor. They'd need suction cups and a hell of a head for heights."

"Some of the guys I met inside? I wouldn't suggest it if I were you."

Walter studied me for a moment. "Whatever happened with you, boy? When you were in college and I was just getting started defending guys in your neighborhood, everyone saw big things."

It was a hell of a question; he was never long on tact, the counsellor from Franklintown. But it was one I'd considered myself a few times. These days, however, things were looking up. I said, "I made my mistakes young enough that I still have time to recover."

"Good to know, my boy. If you ever need any investigative work on the side, you know you can always look me up."

Walter was a busy guy, a lawyer to headline makers. In the prior year alone, he'd had a high-profile armored car crew, the Southside Shouter – a particularly bizarre home invasion specialist who woke his victims in the middle of the night by screaming in their ear – the loan officer accused of the worst case of fraud in Philadelphia banking history, and high-profile sex assault charges against a kids' sports coach.

He was a great guy to shoot the breeze with; but I didn't need him involved. My list of unanswered questions was mounting and Walter snooping around wasn't going to help me figure out why someone would leave thousands of dollars in vintage art behind at a robbery, or how local wise guys might be involved. Or whether they had any connection to the Hecht brothers and their lackey, John DeGoey.

"How are you going to take on the gallery thing as well? You already have a caseload that would tire a cop."

He snorted. "I feel as capable as when I was your age."

"Doesn't it wear you down a little, seeing the same parade of faces over and over again?"

He grinned devilishly. "Not really, my boy. Not so long as the last faces I see are Andrew Jackson, Ulysses S. Grant and Benjamin Franklin."

"All about the Benjamins, isn't it, Walter?"

"Makes the world go round, Liam, my lad," he said. "Makes the world go round."

20.

WALTER HAD TAKEN A CAB over to the restaurant, so I agreed to give him a ride over to his club, where he was meeting his buddies for a bout of competitive drinking, with maybe some poker thrown in for good measure.

The Ivy Club is the kind of place the guys from the Chestnut Hill mansions went when they got lonely in those big empty houses, a white-plaster-and-brick estate-sized building, square as a mathematician. It had been a men's-only club for years – and an exclusive one, at that. But modern times meant new attitudes, which had meant the possible intrusion of ...shudder ... people's wives and visible minorities.

The solution had been to create a clubroom specifically for women, designed by women. They were like two trophy rooms: the trophy husbands in one, the trophy wives in the other.

Still, Walter swore up and down that the weekly Texas hold 'em game upstairs was the best action around. "These guys couldn't tell an inside straight from an inside right, Quinn. You should get in on this," he said, as I pulled up outside the oversized front steps.

"I'm supposed to be turning over a new leaf. Besides, these guys run rich for my blood."

He laughed. "Oh please. The art expert from Fishtown? We are who we are."

Yeah, and if I believed that, Walter would be representing me right now.

"You sure you don't want to come in for a post-lunch snifter?" he said.

"Nah. I told my Ma I'd be working today. The guilt would kill me."

"Suit yourself," he said, as he got out. "Me? I need the odd shot of courage. I know people like to think of me in purely cold, reptilian terms, but there are days..." Then he leaned back through the open window. "Like I said, keep me posted, Liam. There's a lot of work I could throw your way."

There was a certain pragmatic reality to it.

"Hey," I said. "Who's the blonde?"

He turned and looked over his shoulder. It was the same woman I'd seen coming out of Leo Tesser's apartment building. I was pretty sure it was …

"That's Paul Dibartolo's common-law spouse, Monica Lamb," he said. "She's the latest in a string since the departure of the much–lamented Mrs. Dibartolo."

That clinched it. The girl from the picture. "You know he was there the day of the robbery, right?"

Walter looked back over his shoulder again quickly. "Really? I should probably comfort the man."

"Pure class, Walter. The blonde was also walking out of your boy Leo's apartment building yesterday. Heck of a coincidence, that."

"Isn't he dating the gallery curator?"

"Fiancé."

Walter's smile was a mile wide. "Perhaps I misjudged the boy. He might have a future as a lawyer yet."

After dropping him off, I drove home and parked in the underground lot, then took the elevator up to my floor.

Something felt wrong the second I stepped into the hallway, the sensation of imminent danger, boundaries crossed and out of place. I'd seen Ricky just that morning; but he wasn't in the habit of leaving his apartment door open a half-foot. I walked over and gingerly pushed it the rest of the way with my foot.

I went in cautiously, moving slowly down the small corridor that led past his kitchen and into his living room area. He was spending more time than ever these days downstairs at his boyfriend Al's place, so it could have been a robbery without him being home.

"Ricky? You okay buddy?" I said, before peeking around the corner of the living room.

Ricky was sitting in his armchair in a t-shirt and jeans,

shaking with fear. He had a welt above his eye, and given his company, I figured the butt end of a gun for the culprit. The heavy in the other armchair was older, late sixties, neat moustache, balding, in a cheap suit. His partner was a young guy, tanned, immaculate suit, late twenties, standing behind Ricky's chair, gun trained on me.

The older one leaned forward, like a grandfather who wanted to chat, or maybe tell me a story. "Mr. Quinn. Thank you for joining us at last. Your friend here said you'd gone to meet someone for lunch. You sure do take a long time to eat."

"It was Modo Mio. It's this good little…"

The kid waved the gun at me to shut me up, annoyed. "Who you talking to? We know it, okay? Friggin' guy's a restaurant critic."

The older man hand-motioned for him to calm down. "Will you relax? For crying out loud …" He turned his attention back to me. "Sorry about that. And sorry for bumping your friend on the head here, but he got all hysterical like and started screaming and stuff."

"Do you blame him? You guys aren't exactly Ricky's usual social circle."

He smiled thinly. "I got that impression, yeah. Listen, we got an associate wants to talk to you."

"Not an ex-boxer by any chance, sort of slow? Proud he was Golden Gloves once?"

The older guy looked puzzled. "Not that I know of. And I wouldn't suggest it to him, neither. He might take it the wrong way."

That was interesting: it sounded like they weren't with the three jerks who'd tried to work me over earlier. I didn't really have any choice in attending, anyway, given their hardware.

The old guy looked up at his younger associate. "Make

the call, kid," he said.

A few seconds later, the kid was talking rapidly on a cell phone. He hung up. "He'll be here in a few minutes," he said.

Sure enough, after a tense five-minute wait, the older guy led us out of the apartment. As soon as we were in the corridor, he motioned for Ricky to go back inside. "Don't even think about calling the cops, or we'll be back," he said, in a permanent, final tone.

Ricky was still stunned, hesitant. I said, "It's okay, Ricky. Just head on back inside; these gentlemen aren't looking to make any waves." I didn't tell Ricky that if they'd planned on killing me, he'd probably have been dead already. The poor guy was already frightened enough. The term "material witness" wasn't likely to comfort him.

We took the elevator down with one of them on either side. Unlike the guys in the alley, the two of them didn't seem inclined to escalate the threat level; it made sense to wait the situation out and see what was going on.

Outside the building and down the front steps, a black stretch limo had pulled up to the curb. "In," the younger one said. The sidewalk was empty aside from the three us, and a moment later the rear passenger door opened.

21.

The older man got in first and took the far passenger seat. The jump seats were open, and the young guy motioned for me to climb aboard.

Sitting next to the older hood was a familiar, heavy-set figure. His three-piece suit was immaculate, a tightly-knit black wool with dark pinstripes, and his silver-black hair as neat as a magazine cover.

Vin "the Shin" Terrasini had seen his share of newspaper covers, and then some. Or, as he liked to tell his associates, one hundred and twenty-two charges to date … and no convictions.

At eighty-two years of age he'd ruled over the traditional local underworld for two decades. The nickname stemmed from his infamous rod of correction, an iron bar he'd used when he was younger to shatter guys' shins when they couldn't pay their debts.

Allegedly.

"Mr. Quinn. We haven't met."

I nodded in his direction. "Mr. Terrasini."

He smiled, well aware he needed no introduction. "I hear from my associates that you're looking for the two guys who knocked over that gallery."

"Yes, sir. I work for an insurance company. Philadelphia Mutual.

"You're Al Quinn's boy, aren't you?"

That threw me a little. "You know my father?"

He nodded. "The Mighty Quinn. Tough living up to that rep, kid. Good cop. Could have retired much, much earlier, too… if he wasn't such a good cop."

"Nice to hear, sir." Comforting too, after talking to

Norm Esterhaus. And yeah, I called him 'sir'. It wasn't that I wanted to score points in particular; he just scared the Hell out of me.

"You did time with Benny Toes, right?"

Benjamin "Benny Toes" Valiparisi was a Jersey mob guy serving three life sentences for racketeering, extortion and murder. I'd covered his laundry shift a few times and he seemed like a stand-up guy. I just knew him as Benny Toes, and by the time I found out after two weeks that he was *that* guy, I'd already done him a couple of favors, not the least of which was preventing someone from burying a shiv in his back. Consequently, he spent my last year inside trying to even up the score.

Vin the Shin said, "He's my cousin Mario's oldest boy. As you know, things ain't gone so good for him in the last couple of years."

"He's making the best of it, Mr. Terrasini."

"He spoke real highly, kid," he said, as the limo smoothly rolled towards downtown. "I'd been meaning to get one of the boys to look youse up anyhow, see if youse wanted to do some work for us."

That kind of trouble I didn't need. The offer was also the type of thing I could have avoided if I'd never gotten to know Benny Toes. Turning wise guys down was as difficult as getting rid of them once their hooks were in.

"Appreciated, sir. I'm working full-time now but if I ever need a gig, I'll keep it in mind," I said, as non-committal as possible.

Vin the Shin studied me for a minute. "I hear you're a pretty smart kid. So what are you looking for these two for, anyway? I figure a job like this, with no cash up front, that's a pair of meatheads, right there."

"The gallery they knocked over? The manager is a friend of a friend."

"Lady friend?"

"Childhood friend."

"That's good," he said. "Loyalty is a good thing. Rare these days. Listen, you hear anything about these guys, I want to hear about it just as quick."

"Mr. Terrasini, my job, it doesn't allow me to…."

He waved a hand to silence me and shook his head gently. "Don't worry, kid. I'm not going to drag you into this. But I think these two guys are the same two guys who hit one of my places a couple of weeks ago." He saw my surprise and laughed. "Yeah, that was our reaction, too. Robbed the condo I share with my lady friend. Come busting in in the middle of the afternoon."

"Someone robbed you… that's a hell of a surprise, if you don't mind my saying, Mr. Terrasini. Do you mind if I ask what they took?"

Vin the Shin licked his lips, showing a first outward sign of annoyance since we'd started talking. "I had a painting that I had…acquired. I saw it at a showing by a local guy, but he didn't want to sell it. An associate of mine later came into its possession through circumstances known to me, and I had been, let's say, holding onto it for him."

"Should I know the artist?"

He shook his head. "Probably not. Guy named Dufresne."

Again? "It wasn't an oil called *Autumn Mist*, about … 'yay' big, by any chance?" I traced a rectangle in the air.

The mobster's expression turned grave. "You better explain how you know that real quick, Mr. Quinn, or Benny Toes can't put in enough good words for you."

And so I did, up to and including the security tape of the guy fooling with the painting. "But if you had it, that means the one hanging in the gallery was a forgery – and he must have switched the forgery for the real thing … and left the real thing in the gallery."

The old gangster took a deep breath. "That don't make no sense."

"You're telling me."

"Yeah.... well... I don't like that."

"Yes sir..."

"And it ain't good when I don't like stuff, you get me?"

"Yes, Mr. Terrasini." Yeah, I know, I was sucking up like he was dirt and I my name was Dyson. But the guy killed people; it needs to be seen in that context.

"I don't know what these guys are up to, Mr. Quinn, but I'm beginning to become irritated. It would not serve the interests of anyone involved for me to become any more upset. I'm going to rely on you to keep my painting in mind. I might not get it back, but I ain't going to sit around and be disrespected. Am I clear?"

"Crystal, Mr. Terrasini."

He gestured towards the older man. "You need anything, you give Paulie here a call and he'll arrange it."

"Mr. Terrasini, one question..."

"Yeah, kid, what is it?"

"If someone arranged for a copy of the Dufresne painting to be made at some point, for whatever reason, it would help if I could get the name of the artist who painted the copy."

"Why?"

I shrugged. "Can't be that many people who knew there were two versions. It just seems like the percentage place to start."

The mob boss smiled and nodded gently. "Paulie, you made a good call on this kid. Benny Toes was right."

Paulie said, "You got it, Vin."

"Ok, kid, we'll get you a name. But like I said, anything good you get, we want to hear about it."

"Message received," I said.

"Okay." He called up to the driver. "Tommy, pull over here."

They opened the door to let me out. We were a couple of miles, at least, from my building, but I wasn't complaining. After a guy meets with Vin "The Shin" Terrasini, a long walk home beats the hell out of no walk at all.

22.

No doubt, my mother was steamed over Sunday dinner. And she'd be even more upset if she knew I'd skipped church completely.

I thought I'd slide on over to the Druid for an hour or so, have a pint with my dad and survey the damage. Whenever something bothered her, he was both the surrogate whipping boy and the first to hear about it.

Halfway there, my phone rang. I let it go to voicemail, and was going to deal with it later, but after a couple of minutes I had to face that nagging feeling that I was missing something important.

I pulled the Beast off the Vine Street Expressway and checked my messages.

"Hello? Hello? I'm looking for Mr. Quinn. You left a card at the stadium. This is Jeffrey. We talked a little. You bought a couple of beers. At the stadium. Listen, I need to see you again. I... I'm kind of scared, so if you could call me back..."

He left his number and I dialed right away.

"Hello?" The voice was shaky, and the background noise was considerable. I suspected he was at work.

"Jeffrey? It's Liam Quinn. You called me."

A murmured voice in the background, a younger man, said something, but I couldn't make it out.

Jeffrey said, "I can't talk right now. And I'm sorry I called, I can't help you. It was just something stupid," he said.

"Jeffrey, is there somebody there with you?"

The background voice was louder now, almost audible, barking a command.

"No, I ... listen, Mr. Quinn, I'm sorry. I made a mistake."

And then the line went dead.

No doubt that the kid had been scared out of talking to me.

I had an easy time picturing David Mince standing five feet away from his contrite friend, barking threats and orders in equal measure as we talked. It wasn't hard to figure out which one of them had masterminded the beer robbery. I just needed one of them to talk about it on the record, preferably the skinny kid himself.

If one of them folded, the other two would go down quickly. It occurred to me it might be worth getting my father to "stop in" at the booth in full uniform. If the kid was as cold a fish as I thought, it wouldn't intimidate him. But his two frightened friends might start thinking twice.

Mince, on the other hand, was going to take something special. I hadn't yet quite figured out how to deal with his case.

After I got off the phone with the frightened kid, my message light came on. It was Paulie Vincenzo, Terrasini's right-hand man. The Dufresne forger was a small-timer named Polly, a British art student who lived somewhere just across the river in Camden. The guy who'd hired her was dead, but they had the first name, anyway.

I made a mental note to call an old contact from the bad old days and see if he knew more about her work. I had no doubt that Vin the Shin arranged for her to paint the duplicate in the first place, so the name had to be good, which meant she was up to a lot more than just selling easels and watercolor paint-by-numbers. In my experience, a bent nail is a bent nail, and there's always more than one dodge on the go.

But before then, I got back on track for that pint with my father.

The Druid was packed, as it always was on Sunday

afternoon. Plenty of folks in the neighborhood worked a six-day week, so this was their one day of rest. Younger guys were around the pool table, lining up their quarters to claim the next game, and the older guys were already engrossed in debate. Their wives mostly stayed home, thankful for a few minutes of peace and quiet, with the place to themselves.

I move carefully through the near-shoulder-to-shoulder crowd. Michael and Davy were at the bar. I gave them a wave. Mike raised his pint quickly, but Davy shook his head with disdain. I saw him mouth the words "glass coverage" to our civil servant older brother.

My old man must've been out having a smoke, as his stool sat empty between them.

I made my way over to the side doors, out to the makeshift "patio". This time, it was crowded with dad's friends, nearly all former police officers; most of them were silver haired now, laughing, recalling past glorious and the inequities of a world that paid cops less than plumbers.

He was talking to Roman McQueen about something, but stopped when he saw me. In fact, the group stopped as a whole and went silent, an awkward look suggesting I'd just been the topic.

23.

My father's friends weren't exactly my biggest fans. Not anymore. When I was a little kid, they thought I was the homicide department's unofficial mascot. I guess that meant at least one more room full of people I'd disappointed.

"Pa."

He half-heartedly raised his pint my way as a greeting. "Son. I thought you were working all day today. Haven't seen you here on a Sunday in a while, neither."

It was true. Dealing with Davy was tense, which is why I'd been prompting the old man to talk to him.

"You know how it is, Pa. I have to make a living."

"Your mother wasn't real happy at church. She says if you keep missing Sunday dinner, she's going to start giving your portion to Michael."

My brother Michael could eat a whole pork roast on his own. I didn't need him anywhere near mine. Plus, her roast could make an invading army negotiate lasting peace.

"She's playing hardball."

"Hey, you bring this stuff on yourself. She saw you this morning, you know, crossing the street with Walter Beck."

The name drew a round of murmurs from his friends, and one of them spat on the ground dramatically.

"He called me," I said, motioning with my hands for calm. "I'm working a case he's interested in, that's all."

Vic Dubinski chuckled at that. "You hear that, fellas, little Liam's "working a case," like a real copper. Next thing you know, he'll be applying at the academy."

They all had a good laugh at that. They all knew I got out a year earlier. The tips of my father's ears burned red with embarrassment.

Dad said, "Yeah, well he closed more cases than your boy last year," he said. "How's he doing with traffic detail there, Vic?"

Another round of laughs, this time at Vic's expense. They'd do this all day, drinking and trying to out-insult each other. Inevitably, one or two would get too drunk, and the insults would get too personal, and fists would fly for a couple of minutes, a weekly ritual of affirming another week alive, followed by shows of strength.

Vic said, "What are you working on kid?" They ribbed me about prison, but when it came down to it, most of the guys were okay.

"That gallery over on Chestnut... the DeGoey. The painting that was stolen is worth seven figures. Maybe eight."

Vic's buddy Fred Keller whistled low. "That's a lot of scratch for a painting. Must be huge."

I smiled. "It's not so much a size thing. It's actually pretty small."

"Yeah, your wife said," suggested a voice near the back of the crowd.

More laughs. Regular comedians, these guys.

"So... what is it? Is it famous?" Vic said.

"Not really. Just real old, and a particular painter a lot of rich people like," I said.

"I always liked those French guys, what do you call them ...." said Fred. "The impressionists? You know, like the midget?"

"Toulouse Lautrec."

"Yeah, that's the guy. I always liked his work. Like the one with barmaid with the big knockers: real classy."

Getting into the difference between Lautrec and Manet probably wasn't going to score me any points, so I dropped it. Nor was debating Fred's notion of 'classy'.

My father interjected, "So the insurance company you

work for don't want to pay out?"

"What a surprise," said a voice nearby.

Thanks, dad. Real helpful. "No, it's not that. It's just that it's a lot of dough. If there's a way to recover it, they're going to take it, you know?"

Vic worked armed robbery for two decades. "What's the M.O.?" he asked.

"Couple of guys, balaclavas, dark work boots, shotguns. The usual, like you'd see at a bank. We're guessing a driver outside, but he didn't peel out or nothing so there were no tracks."

"No street video?"

"Not a bit."

"And they just took the one painting?"

"Yeah."

"So someone hired them?"

"Yeah, probably. I don't really know. It's a strange one..."

Vic was waiting with bated breath for me to elaborate, but my dad cut me off. "Now, enough of that stuff. You mugs are retired! Liam, don't go stirring up the boys. They ain't going to let Vic re-up at his age."

The guys dispersed from our little group. But Fred had worked bunko for years and I held him back for a moment when everyone else went inside. "You might be able to help me a little," I told him. "You only retired last fall, right?"

Fred took a sip of beer and sighed. "Yeah, finally hung it up. Still wondering about going back. What's the deal?"

"I'm not sure this is just a robbery."

"Eh?"

"It's bizarre, Mr. Keller. But there's some kind of tie to a forger named Polly. That ring any bells?"

He thought about it. Fred was in his early sixties, but he still had a bright memory for perps. "Yeah. Yeah, it's familiar.

She's the Brit, right? She was Pat Delaney's old lady, last time I heard. Has an arts store in Jersey. We had her on a check-washing job a few years back, but the chain of evidence got messed up."

The chain is the series of evidence-gathering protocols police follow to ensure material can't be tainted and effectively remains neutral. It means the stuff has to be bagged and tagged with rubber gloves at the time it's found, then sealed and held in a locked evidence room, so no one can mess with it. And check washing is an old scam: the forger gets a genuine check for a small amount from the victim – either from an in-person sale that is then passed onto them or by stealing it from their trash. They then use chemicals to wash off the name and few numbers, which they replace with their preference. If it's used, they take out the cancellation stamp as well.

"What happened?"

He shook his head. "We were never sure. Drove your old man out of his freakin' mind, though."

I said, "You hear anything more recent about her?"

"I've been retired three months, Liam, I don't hear that much no more," said Fred.

"But you said she "was" Pat Delaney's lady? She's not now?"

"Nah, he's inside, doing a dime for trying to knock over a Brinks truck just over a year ago."

I'd seen the story in the papers at the time. Three guys in clown masks had used a timed charge to blow out the vehicle's axle when it slowed down to pay the toll on the Ross Bridge to Jersey. They'd piled out of the car behind it, laid down the toll booth attendant and the drivers on the cement, blown the doors off the back with another charge.

It was quick, bloodless, professional.

But the second his two accomplices finished loading the

cash into the car, the driver of the getaway car had taken off and left them behind. They'd jumped from the bridge to escape the cops, and were thought to have been swept away in the Delaware River. The water was so cold, they shouldn't have lasted more than five or ten minutes.

A toll camera caught Delaney, a nogoodnik from the neighborhood, from a side profile behind the wheel of the car. Cops picked him up two days later in Camden, pulling him out of bed in the middle of the night with a full SWAT team.

"Pat Delaney," I said. "Wow. There's a name from the past. My dad busted him a bunch of times. You know Delaney at all?"

He nodded. "Yeah, from when I worked robbery. He hung around with this stocky side of beef, guy named Teddy Armas. Real loud mouth, likes throwing his fists around. Doesn't discriminate between male and female."

"About five-eight, brags about being Golden Gloves back before time?"

He laughed. "Yeah, that sounds like him. Might have been the only guy we liked less than Pat. Never seemed to have nothing on him. Why?"

"If he's the guy I think, he's not much of a fighter. But I'm guessing he can swim some."

"You're joking."

"He sure didn't look too dead to me, not when he was trying to throw big bombs at my head. He has some friends working with him, too."

"Then you're thinking Delaney's tied to your robbery somehow?"

"Something like that. Like you said, he's still inside. But he's a neighborhood guy; he's got friends on the outside."

"But why a gallery? What, he owes someone inside a favor, maybe?"

"That's the money question, Mr. Keller. I figure that out and maybe this month I make some myself."

"Well I hope you do, Liam," he said. "I always thought you were a good kid, you just messed up some, that's all."

"Thanks, Mr. Keller."

"You still seeing that girl? You know: the pretty redhead with the dark skin?"

Guys of Mr. Keller's age aren't always big on the sensitivities. "Nora? Nah, just friends. We go way back and believe me, she's pure class – way above a pug like me. I mean... seriously out of my league."

He studied me for a minute. He was a picture of weathered creases and balding silver hair, more years than most of us can imagine, many more than his actual age. "Don't sell yourself so short. My wife is the most beautiful woman I ever saw, and I look like a hung-over frog." He held up a hand to stop me from protesting. "Don't bother, kid, I know I ain't pretty. But she loves me right anyhow."

And like I said: It's a tight neighborhood.

My father had drifted back to the bar, and both Davy and Mike had taken off home. I took the stool next to him and ordered a Rolling Rock.

He took a hefty pull on his Straub before wiping his top lip with the back of his hand. "So, was Freddy any help?"

"He knew the person I was looking for. Turns out she was one of Pat Delaney's old ladies."

His eyes rolled up for a second. "Really narrows it down some."

"Listen, Pa, I ran into an old partner of yours today, guy named Norm Esterhaus. You never mentioned him none that I recall."

When my father's unhappy, his poker face is pretty much non-existent. He takes on a grim look and lets it hang there, waiting for someone to break the uncomfortable silence. "So what? You got a question, Liam?"

"Why didn't you mention him?"

He drained his glass and took a deep breathe. "Some things are best left in the past and he's one of those things. We wasn't partners for too long, let's put it that way."

"You had a falling out, or what?"

He stared at me sideways again. "You need to analyze my feelings, Liam? Leave it be, okay?"

When my father wanted to stop talking about something, he made that pretty obvious, too.

Besides, I had more pressing issues than my father's ex-partner – like why someone would return an original painting to a gallery at the same moment they were busy stealing a classic Vermeer worth millions, thirty feet across the room.

24.

I WAS WORKING ON the speed bag, hands moving in a blur, pace increasing steadily as my bicep muscles strained and the sweat began to form, the city lights shining bright at night through my apartment window.

One of the great things about boxing is that even when you're not actually competing, you still get to beat the Hell out of an inanimate object. When things aren't going so good, I take solace in that.

The phone rang.

I'd be a liar if I didn't say I hoped it was Nora. She'd been on my mind pretty much non-stop since the soccer match, and I knew she'd had as good a time as I had. I'd spent a part of the day going through stupid fantasy scenarios in which she suddenly realized I was the right guy, right under her nose all along.

I know… it was kind of sad. Still, when you're moony over someone, every time the phone rings it's potentially them.

I grabbed the cordless.

No such luck.

"Mr. Quinn? It's Jeffrey? Jeffrey Tillis? From McFinnigans, at the stadium?" Like a lot of kids, his voice trailed up at the end, a subconscious tendency towards insecurity that made every statement sound a little like a question.

"Hey Jeffrey. Where are you?" I wanted to dominate the conversation, use his nervousness to pin him down for a meeting.

"I… uh…what?"

"Where are you? We should get coffee and talk in person."

"I'm... I'm at home with my parents."

"Okay. Is there a coffee shop or something near you?"

"Uh.... yeah. Yeah! It's, like, six blocks south of here..."

He gave me address, and twenty minutes later we were sitting across from each other in the orange vinyl back-corner booth, away from the big windows at the front of the place. The young man's eyes scanned the room every few seconds, although it was empty except for the counter clerk.

"Nervous?"

"Yeah. I guess, maybe. My friends don't really come in here."

"Do you consider David Mince a friend?" I nodded towards his arm. "That burn doesn't look particularly friendly."

His eyes were still nervous, but Jeffrey was inquisitive, too. "How did you know that was a cigarette burn? Were you really in jail?"

"Nothing exciting or glamorous about it. Prison is Hell. The worst. I keep in pretty good shape and I've been training as a fighter for a lot of years, but I had to watch myself every second, Jeffrey."

He nodded but didn't say anything.

I said, "Another thing you get to recognize in jail is when someone has what they call "dead eyes," when they're a real sociopath, and the most dangerous."

"Like David."

"Exactly like David. When he burned you with that cigarette, was DeShawn there?"

He nodded.

"Is DeShawn sort of slow?"

He looked down, like he didn't want to speak ill of him. "He doesn't realize when things are serious. He's kind of like a big kid. I don't think it's his fault or anything. He's not stupid, not really. He was just born … you know, delayed."

"And they helped someone rob the restaurant?"

He nodded again. The kid's embarrassment at being even tangentially involved was acute. I figured it spoke well of whoever raised him.

"How do you guys know each other?"

"We all go to school together. Well, sort of. We've all been going less lately."

"You go back a ways?"

"Yeah."

"David's always been the leader?"

He nodded. "Yeah, I guess."

"Did he make you get a job at the stadium?"

He shook his head. "No, I started working there first. He and DeShawn, they only came on after I started there. I… I guess I didn't see what he was like, not at first."

"But then you started seeing problems?"

"The till came up short a bunch of times, always when David was on. And I caught him spitting in the soup of the day. But he straight up told me that DeShawn would do anything he asked him to do, that they were like brothers, and that if I said anything, he'd have me put in hospital."

"Were you there when the robbery happened?"

"No," he said sullenly. "David tried to bring me along and I said I was going to go to the cops. That's when he got DeShawn to hold me down and he burned me."

"David had older friends who picked up the beer?"

He nodded again. "David had a copy of my key to the storage area made. Then they hid out in the restaurant, so they wouldn't have to swipe their security cards to get in again. He said his older brother is in a gang. But then I heard he doesn't really have one, he just lied about it, like everything else." He looked up nervously at me. "If they knew I was talking to you…"

I raised my palm. "Don't worry, okay? You won't have to talk to me again until after it's been dealt with. Just pretend we didn't talk."

He gave a smile of half-reassurance and nodded. I got up to go.

"Just be patient and try and avoid them. Take some time off work if you can; I'll make sure they don't hold it against you."

"Mr. Quinn… he really, genuinely scares me. I mean… I know I'm not supposed to admit that and all…"

"A man without fear is a fool," I suggested. "That's your instinct telling you to take action to help yourself, though… and that's what you've done. So trust me with his, okay? I'll get back to you, Jeffrey. You know where I am if you need me."

He smiled again but didn't say anything. At the counter, I grabbed another small coffee. The waitress glanced back once at the kid, then at me, her dour looking making me wonder what she was thinking. Probably something dark and disappointing.

Then I headed back into the tepid city evening.

25.

I put on my best middle-aged Chicago Bears fan accent as I sat in the West Philadelphia church's confession booth.

"Bless me, fadder, for I have sinned. It has been four hunnert-and-tirty-two-days since my last confession."

A pause. "That's… an interesting accent. What can I help you with this evening, my son?"

"Fadder, my wife… she don't like it when I stuff too much knockwurst inta my fat yap. Can you bless my colon, so's I can enjoy a reasonable share of pork and pork products on gameday?"

Nothing. Not a sound.

The curtain to the booth was yanked open, the sudden movement designed to prevent me from fleeing before discovery. "You're nearly forty and you're still a juvenile delinquent."

My brother Andy is a priest. He's the most patient, forgiving member of my family... and he's still a total hardass. But he's also good people. He knows any number of secrets about the residents of this city and he's not going to share them with me. He's also a repository of forty-six years of public life in Fishtown, where he still travelled every night, to his one-bedroom apartment a few blocks from my parents' house.

I held up both hands in surrender. "Please, fadder... don't touch me in the bad way...."

"Get out of the booth, ya jackass," he ordered.

I joined him, still chuckling at his discomfort.

"This is a serious thing, what I do," he said. He waved his arm around the church for a moment, to accentuate its size and the gravity of it all.

"I do get that, really," I said. "But I so like the pork and the pork products, fadder..."

"What do you want, Liam? It's eight-thirty at night. I'm leaving for home in thirty minutes and I still have things to take care of."

At least with Andy I didn't get a lecture about my evil jailbird ways. "You're always following the neighborhood news. I need everything you know about Pat Delaney."

Pat Delaney was semi-famous in Fishtown – or maybe 'notorious' would be more suited. He was six or seven older than me, in Andy's class in school.

Not that Pat was big on the spirit of education – if

Jeffrey Tillis thought he was having attendance problems, he just had to talk to Pat on visiting day to get an idea of where dropping out of school could lead.

Andy sighed. "Pat Delaney. There's a blast from the past, right there. He never had it easy. His father, Gerry? A cold man. He wasn't a big guy, just strong as iron from working the docks his whole life, a seething bundle of jail tats with a scowl and a goatee. He had as violent a cruel streak as ever crossed the ocean to make a buck."

"A real bad guy."

He nodded. "Pa arrested him a bunch of times over the years and there was no love lost between the two families. But Pat had it real hard. He ran away from home in junior high, and was living off petty crime full time, in and out of the joint constantly."

"Part of the system."

"He had a big -- if uninspiring -- collection of court appearances, beginning with assault at eighteen, two years for smashing another kid in the face with a half-full vodka bottle."

People see other people get hit with bottles in the movies and they think it's no big thing; but bottle glass is thick and heavy, and you're lucky if all it does it shatters and cuts you up horribly. If it doesn't, it breaks every bone in your face, or ruptures your skull and kills you deader than a coffin nail.

"The kid in question was Amish and on "Rumspringa," Andy explained. "That's a period where Amish kids leave the nest to test out the larger society. Pat ran into him in Washington Park and demanded his wallet. The kid needed forty-three stitches and suffered a broken cheek bone. And after that, there was no doubt about whether the Amish kid wanted to stay in the city."

It wasn't Philly's proudest moment, nor something

uncommonly terrible. I remembered the TV news had 'before' and 'after' images of the kid: with friends just a month earlier, blonde and curly haired, innocently smiling; and a year later, outside court, a sullen, broken individual, with sunken eyes and pronounced cheekbones, his emotional security as shattered and jagged as the scar that ran down his jawline, from his ear to his chin.

"After that, Pat moved on to a check kiting beef, then to knocking over the odd bank or family business. He got nailed for a liquor store robbery."

"You think he'd have learned after that stretch."

"You might think. Instead, as soon as he got out, he proceeded to try to knock over a Brinks truck with two friends. I'm going to figure he spent twenty-five of his forty-five or forty-six years on this planet in the stir."

The judge in the case, a noted lightweight when it came to sentencing, had said he didn't believe Delaney's story that most of the money had washed away in the Delaware along with his two friends, because a distant bridge camera showed them loading objects into the car. But he still gave him credit for not actually succeeding, a move the district attorney's office publicly denounced.

Now, don't get me wrong: I've done time, so I have sympathy for how young people can get excited, and caught up, and make mistakes. And once you're in the system, it's an absolute freak show, a marketplace of misery and malevolence.

But Pat wasn't a bonehead; he was a vicious by-product of a vicious household, and he was best kept inside the pen, where civil people weren't at risk.

If his old crew was still around and up to no good? The next time I ran into them, I wouldn't forget to keep my back to the wall.

26.

As likely as it seemed that Pat Delaney was involved in the gallery heist, I couldn't rule out the possibility that the owner, John DeGoey, or his crooked business partner, Dennis Hecht, were somehow as well.

Then there was another player: the artist, Clinton Dufresne, who'd both been there on the day of the robbery and was the subject of the thieves' sleight-of-hand.

Dufresne worked and sold art directly from his loft downtown. At six-feet-seven inches tall, he'd been an NCAA first-team small forward for St. John's. But Dufresne gambled on himself; he rolled the dice and came up a winner, giving up basketball to pursue his art. First, he got a degree in architecture, and won awards as an up-and-comer with astonishing taste.

Then he stunned the local fine arts world, producing eclectic-but-deeply-emotional abstracts in oils, as well as clay sculptures reminiscent of Henry Moore.

The elevator opened directly into his large, open-concept space — yet another factory conversion — and Dufresne greeted me with a confident handshake. He reminded me vaguely of a young Sidney Poitier, with that same intensity, only Dufresne also wore small round Lennon specs and had a small goatee, like a bigger, stronger Sean Combs. The glass in them seemed thin, and I wondered whether he actually had bad eyesight, or just his own sense of style.

"I was surprised when you called me, Mr. Quinn."

"Just routine. I'm talking to everyone who was there."

"I'm glad. It's easy to be sensitive in this town…"

"How do you figure?"

"Well," he said, "you know."

"About?" I thought I did, but these days you have to be careful. I mean, we always should have been but... I digress.

"You know how it is: Philly cops and the black community have some history. Some really, really bad history."

True enough. I was alive for the satchel bombing of MOVE, a black political group, by the police in Nineteen Eighty-Five. Eleven people had been killed in one of the most egregiously violent and racist attacks on Americans in the history of law enforcement. My father still wore it with shame, even though he hadn't been involved. The fact that his department had done something so insanely dangerous and crooked still ate at him, years later.

"You grew up here?"

"Yeah, north side. My parents have a little bookstore and coffee shop off East Wadsworth, the Island Sun."

"Jamaican?"

He laughed. "Jah, mon." Then he dropped the pretense, his caramel-soft tone returning. "But that's their generation, not mine."

The loft was an impressive blend of his pieces and art he loved, an eclectic jumble of modern and surreal, from the ribbon-like spiral light fixture to the free-form sofa, to the pop-art cartoon mishmash that hung above his desk like an explosion of Roy Lichtenstein worship. It was inspiring, but also worrisome. He was young and patrons were obviously throwing money at him; I knew from personal experience that it could go south.

Then I cursed myself internally, for having the audacity to compare his legitimate self-expression with forgeries. If I was thinking like that, even for a second, I knew I obviously still had a lot to learn.

Dufresne, on the other hand, was relaxed and

comfortable. But I think he noticed my awe at his taste and collection.

"Let's go get a coffee downstairs. There's a nice little place on the main floor..." he said, before gesturing around him. "It's a little less ... 'work' down there."

In the cafe, we grabbed a booth by the tinted front window. The building was an old factory conversion, and they'd take the opportunity to tap a Forties and Fifties sense of style inside the restaurant. The books were black vinyl and each white-topped table had a small push-button jukebox attached to a wall bracket under the adjacent window.

He nursed a black coffee, listening intently while I filled him in – generally – on what I knew. I didn't mention the thieves messing around with his picture.

It turned out I didn't have to.

"That's the one thing," he said when I'd wrapped up. "That was the one thing was really strange about the whole robbery: my work was crooked. When we were all done and they'd fled with the Vermeer, it was sticking out like a sore thumb."

"You noticed at the time?"

"Yeah, man... ego can be a bitch sometimes, for sure. But I'm an artist, so I'm practically demanding props on a regular basis, you know? First thing I did when I walked in there was check out my own stuff. And that frame was perfectly straight originally."

"Not the only thing, surely?" He looked puzzled. I said, "The fact that they didn't steal anything other than the one painting."

"Oh. Yeah, I guess." He squinted, the puzzling nature of it hitting him. "What's that about?"

He didn't seem at all disingenuous. He would notice his own work, of course. I sure would have. But he was also the only person -- other than me -- who'd thought it significant, and that also suggested he wasn't involved. A good thief might, as they say, help you look for the wallet he stole; but he never leads you towards his own back pocket.

I asked, "So what were you thinking took place, Mr. Dufresne? You got an angle on this whole thing I haven't thought of yet, maybe? Because, I'll tell you straight out, right now I feel like a toddler lost in the Poconos. I ain't even sure which way is up."

He thought about it for a minute. "From the sound, I'd say they switched paintings. And... again, man, it's Clinton. None of this 'mister' stuff."

I smiled. At least he wasn't full of himself. That put him in the better half of successful artists I'd known. "But... they didn't, right? I'm guessing you got up real close to it..."

Dufresne grinned broadly. "Yeah... I'm not so overloaded with projects that I don't recognize my own brush strokes. It was the real thing, for sure."

"You checked closely?"

"Right after the robbery. As soon as I noticed it was crooked, I hustled over there. I was about to straighten it, but the old security guard yelled at me not to touch it. Then he told yelled for everyone to stay put and not touch anything, as it was evidence."

He may not have been paid enough to risk his life, but at least the guard had done something right. "And when you first entered the gallery?"

He squinted again. "I don't understand the question."

"Was there anything amiss with your piece when you first came in?"

Dufresne was thinking hard. "I ... don't..."

"You're not sure, are you?"

He shook his head, looking a little worried. "I didn't look closely. I saw it from across the room and they'd positioned it just... well, just perfectly for the space. I was genuinely impressed, as the overall esthetics of an exhibition seem to escape so many exhibitors and galleries."

"But you didn't walk over then, initially, as you did later?"

He shrugged. "It wasn't crooked. I noted its excellent show position, and that got me thinking I could convince DeGoey or Alison Pace to carry a couple of more pieces. I turned away at that point and sought her out. I guess I got distracted by business."

"Understandable. So after the robbery, it was definitely your painting. But before…"

He frowned. "Mr. Quinn … you got any idea what's going on here?"

"Not sure yet … and it's Liam."

The waitress came over and he ordered us another round of coffee. "But 'not sure' means you have some idea," said Dufresne.

"I have … the beginnings of an idea," I said. "What I do know is that the picture you saw after the robbery was the original – but they did switch it, for a copy that had been hanging in its place. Whoever pulled this all off, it's some confusing jawn they got working, some grift."

Dufresne had a sudden look of shock on his face, like someone realizing they've just missed an essential appointment, or a family member's birthday. "My gallery, it was hit a couple of years ago. We thought it was just a smash and grab for cash …"

"They didn't take anything else?"

He shook his head. "I didn't think so, but…" Dufresne looked embarrassed. "That means it sat there for months without me realizing…" He averted his eyes to the floor, mortified. "Oh God… Oh Lord, I am so embarrassed I can't even look at you."

I tried to comfort him. "Look, Clinton: you have to

realize that the guys who do this for a living ... well, they're like expert handwriting forgers, ensuring the right weight on every loop, the right lean on every letter. This is what they do, make perfect copies. Perfect usually to all but the utmost discerning, studious eye. They're meticulous down to the brush stroke, down to every flake of paint they can replicate. Down to the age of the canvas or paper, if they can find something contemporaneous to work with when fleecing somebody."

He stared at me with a look that bordered on concern, or maybe sadness. "Liam, if I didn't know better from what you're trying to accomplish, it would sound almost like you respect them.

I smiled awkwardly. "It's my former trade. I served three years for forging Japanese masters."

For a second, it was like he was looking right through me. Then he said, "And they let you be an investigator? After you did time?"

I nodded. "A friend of a friend is a former high-ranking policeman and a colleague of the mayor. He put in a word and I was given a provisional license. It won't become permanent and my firearms prohibition won't be lifted for ten years. Even then, on the latter, I have to apply for an exemption."

"Huh."

The look on his face wasn't one of admiration that I was taking my punishment and deterrent hardships so well. "That doesn't sit right with you?" Because it sure felt like being a social outcast from where I was sitting.

He shook his head. "Not really. I'm proud of myself for doing well. But I see a lot of other young dudes who haven't made it yet, who haven't risen above the tough lot they were handed in life. And if they made that one mistake, and went up for forgery? Wouldn't anyone be giving them a job as an investigator afterwards, Liam. Not if you're black in this town."

What was I going to do, argue with him? I knew the stats, the record of inequities in sentencing despite equivalent arrest rates for things like drug dealing and prostitution, the community divides.

"You're right," I said. "But don't think just because you had it the worst that the rest of us had it easy. I grew up in Fishtown in the bad old days, when it was the white trash equivalent of west Philly. Wasn't any gentrification back then, and those boys were tough. If you were an Irish Catholic kid with no money, you didn't get a silver spoon. Same with the Poles and the Russians, anyone who wasn't some rich WASP kid. I also know it's a lot worse for minorities. I can't change that."

"As long as you acknowledge reality, man… that's all any of us can ask most of the time. Most people decent – most people not the problem," he said.

"But just so you know," I added, "it wasn't racism that got me a license or white privilege. It was nepotism. My boss is my best friend's father."

He looked down and shook his head. "Look man… I'm sorry if I get hot over it, but you know the history. Race has been a tough dividing line in this town, a deadly one."

"Hey, I'm no dummy. I know I got breaks. But I also work real hard to make the most of them. I don't take anything for granted no more, Clinton.

Dufresne smiled. "I'm sure you don't. It's hard inside, isn't it?"

I nodded. "You did time?"

"As a juvenile, so nothing like what you had to deal with. But my cousin is in for life. He got caught up in a gang beef, shot a guy who was going to shoot him. I've heard tell from him about it being just about the worst place you could be on this Earth, a confined guerilla warzone."

"It could be like that, yeah. I met a lot of very, very bad people in CFCF. But I also met some real stand-up guys, too, guys like me who'd made a mistake young, justified things to themselves because of emotional immaturity. A lot of them, they're just kids with bad parents and ADHD who are still twelve years old on the inside but twenty-something on the outside. Until one catches up with the other, they keep exhibiting poor impulse control, poor judgement. If they're lucky, nobody gets seriously hurt and they get on with life eventually, once they've figured out how not to be a selfish little prick."

He thought about that. "I never really considered it like that but.. yeah, that matches a lot of what I saw – and some of how I behaved -- growing up. I still… I just have a hard time with the fact that someone could copy my art perfectly to begin with. That's… it's like saying they could copy my soul."

"And that's why they're never perfect, just as close as copy can get. You shouldn't beat yourself up. Every line, every daub, every crease. They're that good. There's always something missing, if the right person looks, precisely because of what you're describing, the intangible that made the original artist the great creator, not the meticulous fraud."

He sighed. "Easy to say, man. But I exhibited a fake of my own painting for over a year. That kind of thing could make me a laughingstock. Now I wish I'd just sold the damn thing when I had a chance."

That was interesting. I wondered why he'd held onto something so immediately lauded after it had displayed publicly. "You had offers?"

"Yeah, two potential buyers. One was a call-in that didn't want his employer identified…"

I interrupted. "And the other was a young British

woman, mid-twenties?"

His eyes widened. "How...?"

"The first buyer was a gangster who wanted the painting. Don't ask which one; it wouldn't be good for your health to know. The second was the girl who painted the copy for one of his associates when you wouldn't sell."

Wistful, Dufresne downed another swallow of coffee and slumped back in his seat. "And I turned down all that cash," he said.

"There's an upside," I offered.

"Oh?"

"Well, sure. You have the real one back. Put it in a safety deposit box, and the next time someone offers more than you think it's worth? Take the money."

"Guaranteed to keep hoodlums off my back?"

"Absolutely. Or so I'm told. And you know what? They're like DeGoey: they have egos, too. They'll feel compelled to show it off, to let other people enjoy it."

I finished off my coffee and got up to go. "Look, if you think about anything else that might help ..."

"Sure, sure..." Then he looked puzzled again. "That thing you said, about the Vermeer being the only painting taken, that's interesting."

"How so?"

Dufresne downed his coffee and got up to join me. "Well, if it was just about the value of the paintings, they'd have stolen as many as possible, and they wouldn't have taken a copy of my work. That means it wasn't about hurting DeGoey. The best way to do that would've been to strip the place clean. He couldn't have handled the insurance losses. There were two distinct agendas at work here: one to steal a painting, the other involving my piece."

"And if it's not about the insurance damage that also means it's not about an oversized claim," I said. "That means someone had a market for the one work and the other was… something else. It makes it even less likely anyone there that day was connected. Multiple agendas mean multiple people who know things, loose lips."

Clinton was asking some of the same questions I'd been asking for two days. But the puzzled expression on his face spoke volumes. "I don't get it, Liam. It doesn't make any sense."

If I'd had answers for him, I'd have offered them.

27.

The phone rang just after I'd gotten home.

I was sitting on one of the bar stools at the kitchen island, watching a politician on TV explain why America's economic problems were the fault of the unionized working man and laziness– and apparently failing to notice the bit where people worked eight hours longer now than forty years ago for an inflation-adjusted lower income. The greedy bastards were stealing all the money. He missed that part.

I answered. "Quinn."

The woman's aging Irish lilt hadn't lessened after five decades in America. "And is this how you answer the phone!? So rude and abrupt like, without a hint of welcome or common courtesy? And how is that a civil way to be behaving?"

It didn't do to be abrupt with Maureen Dahmnait Iris Quinn.

"Ma... Sorry, I..."

"Oh, sure and you're sorry today. But you weren't sorry enough last night to call and tell me you were missing dinner yourself. Don't sorry me, you ungrateful boy!"

My mother has been in America since age fourteen. She sounds like she moved from Derry last Tuesday.

I needed this like a tax hike. "Ma, I'm sorry, really..."

"Don't tell me you're sorry. Look in the mirror, because we had your favorite: chicken and dumplings."

She knew exactly where to hurt a guy. "Dumplings... really?"

It just came out, instinctive like.

"Don't worry. I saved you some in a microwavable dish,

although it's not as good as when it's fresh."

"Awww… thanks, Ma. I love you."

"I love you, too, dear," she said. "What was so important that you couldn't be here to have dinner with your family? And to miss church, no less! You may say you love me, but you didn't show much love for the Lord this past weekend."

"I told Dad, I had to work," I said, regretting it instantly. They bickered constantly, and she'd be using that little piece of information against him later, probably after he got home late from the pub.

Then I'd hear it back from him, at length, probably with one of my older brothers chiming in, as a way to suck up to my father.

"Oh, you did, did you? Well we'll be having words when he gets home tonight."

Yeah. Great. "Ma…"

"Don't 'Ma' me, Liam Conor Sean Quinn. I was really disappointed! Davy finally seemed like he might open up and talk to you again, give a little bit in this whole dispute you've got, and you decide not to show."

Yeah, when pigs flew. She wishfully thought he might change his mind just about every week.

"Ma, I could come home with St. Peter's halo and…"

"Liam, don't blaspheme!"

"Ma…."

By the time we got off the phone after twenty minutes, she'd not only gotten me to practically sign a contract in blood that I'd come to Sunday dinner the next weekend, she'd also managed to load up on the guilt by pointing out how proud she was of my success with PMI.

Yeah, I know. She's a great mom.

And that got me thinking. The news had finished in the background and the sports had come on, including a preview of the next Union game.

It occurred to me that a kid like DeShawn, with some problems… well, he might just have a mom who'd want to know about his time hanging around David Mince, a mom who'd want to keep him out of trouble, If she knew what he was getting up to at work.

It was early evening, but I gambled I could get hold of Terence Bryson. I fished his card out of my wallet. A few minutes later, I was pulling him away from the television.

"You realize the Phillies are on, right?"

"Yeah, I'm sorry about that, Mr. Bryson. Do you have a home address on DeShawn Ellis?

He sighed. "Give me a few minutes."

It was time to find up what Jeffrey Tillis was up against, and whether I could put Mike Murphy's beer case to bed.

28.

DeShawn Ellis lived in West Philly, which can be rough.

The building looked like it should be illegal. Several outside windows were boarded up. I did a walk around – I like to know where I might find myself stuck – and it looked like the back door was sealed shut, too, which was definitely against fire code.

The balconies were half hanging off the building and several were full of debris and trash.

Surprisingly, the lobby was nicer. It may have been illegal and neglected, but the residents were keeping the inside of the former tenement in as close to passing condition as possible.

Mailbox 312 had half a name tag sticker, but enough to identify it as the Ellis family's place. I walked up the three short flights cautiously; West Philly can be tough as the best of times, and you never knew who you might run into in a big building, bolting down a flight of stairs at top speed.

The plaster on the corridor walls was flaking, patched over and mottled; a remnant of the building's best days, probably back just after the Second World War. The tenants had valiantly tried to mask it with bright white paint, but like the rest of the building it was never going to look optimistically new again; the scars ran too deep.

I knocked on their door. A young girl of perhaps four or five in white pajamas answered. "Mom!" she yelled, without asking me who I was. She walked back into the apartment leaving the door open a crack. Then I heard her mother's hurried voice. "Tonya, what did I tell you about leaving that door open?"

She peeked through the gap, obviously surprised by me.

"Can I help you. sir?" she asked formally.

"Mrs. Ellis? My name is Liam Quinn. I'm working for the folks over at the stadium, in Chester."

"You want to talk to DeShawn? He's not here."

"No ma'am ... actually, I was hoping to talk to you."

She looked at me suspiciously. "So then... uh... if I call the folks at the Stadium, they'll know who you are?"

The woman needed confidence I wasn't trying to trick her. "I can wait outside if you like. Ask for Terence Bryson. He's the security guy."

She nodded knowingly. "I met him when I took DeShawn down for his interview." She opened the door, eyeing me warily. "I guess you should come on in."

Mrs. Ellis led me into a small, plain two-bedroom. The living room was neat and tidy, with family pictures the main decoration, a pair of small couches and an armchair. There were some toys by the coffee table, and she shushed her daughter towards them. "Sweetie, you pick up your stuff and take them to your toy box."

"You have a lovely home, Mrs. Ellis."

She looked unimpressed. "I guess. We try, but I guess you saw how the building is."

"Tough getting some landlords to do their job."

"Uh-huh."

The little girl was standing behind her mother's leg now, half peeking around at me, and she smiled and grabbed her doll, along with its bright pink house, and headed down the adjacent corridor.

She watched the girl depart then returned her attention to me. "Now... have a seat there on the sofa. What can I do for you, Mr. ... sorry, what did you say the name was again?"

"Quinn, Ma'am, Liam Quinn."

I sat down and she took the adjacent armchair. I filled her in on her son's recent troubles. "I think this other kid

David Mince has been filling your son's head with a lot of pretty dangerous stuff. He might even have involved him in the robbery and he's definitely using him for muscle."

To say Mrs. Ellis appeared unhappy would be an understatement. She looked like … well, an angry mom, I guess. And everyone – but everyone – knows what that can be like.

"Where you say this boy David is? Where would you think he might be right now?"

"Mrs. Ellis…"

She turned her head slightly, haughtily, as if measuring up her next necessary statement. "Mr. Quinn, my boy is a good boy. He's just a little slower than some. He's not simple, he just takes a different view of things, and takes a little longer to get there, that's all. In fact, I expect there are some folks people think of as normal and smart who aren't as bright as he can be. Every couple of years, there's some other boy, usually an older boy, who takes advantage of him. But I don't let that go by. Maybe I should speak to his mother…"

"No… ma'am, please… what I need you to do is simple: forbid him from working at the stadium anymore."

She looked a little embarrassed. "Look, my husband passed away last year, and I have two other children to raise. We need his income in the household, Mr. Quinn. I wish I could say it wasn't so, but right now…"

I'd hoped she would just agree to keep him away and remove all of Mince's influence. Then something struck me. I grabbed a piece of scrap paper from inside my wallet and passed her the address. "Have him meet me here next Sunday, and I'll have a better job for him. It'll pay the same, or better, but he won't have the travel costs."

She took the address. "You sure?"

"Mrs. Ellis, like I said: I already have enough evidence to pass on to the police so that they can nab David Mince, as long as he's honest about everything that happened."

"He will be. I'll see to that. As long as…"

"I have no reason to make it up. Just have him come around 6 p.m. Okay?"

I figured she was about a decade older than me, but the toll of raising three kids in a tough town had taken its toll; she might've been younger than I thought, maybe even younger than me. "Mr. Quinn…. Okay. I'm going to call your Mr. Bryson tomorrow morning and check up on you, but if you're straight up, we'll take you up on that."

Things were looking up. I might have just solved two problems in one, I thought. It hadn't helped me find the forger or the painting, but it was one less headache.

Clinton Dufresne had put the focus squarely back where it belonged, on the lone element of the robbery that seemed inexplicable: replacing a forgery hanging on the gallery wall with the real thing.

There had to be a hell of a motive: beyond staging the Vermeer theft, the thieves had also robbed Vin the Shin in order to get the original back, which was either the bravest thing they could ever do or the dumbest. In my eyes, it verged towards the latter. But either way, there had to be a big payoff for a man – any man, no matter how crazy – to cross the local head of the Mafia.

But why? Why stage a robbery to return a valuable painting?

The only two people I figured might have the answer were Pat Delaney and his old lady, Polly. He was going to be behind bars for a few years and, I was acutely aware, was going to take some sweet talking from Walter before he'd talk to the likes of me.

That left me with one option: I had to find the woman.

29.

I knew Pat Delaney's ex-old lady had been named Polly, and that she worked out of Jersey. If she spent a lot of time in Philly, then Camden or Cherry Hill seemed likely.

And that was all I knew. In other words, not much.

I tried the path of least resistance first, stopping by the public library and searching the newspaper database for terms like "convicted", "forgery", "personation", and the name Polly. Sometimes the papers find something interesting in a case and, as a course of the trial, pick up personal information about the accused.

No such luck. I didn't doubt she had priors if she hung around with Pat, but they weren't for anything worth making the evening news.

I wasn't sure where to take it next; I knew a few street-level guys – associates of Danny Saint, mostly – but they weren't into that level of business.

So instead, I waited until I was outside the library branch and I reluctantly called someone I hadn't called in four years.

"I don't recognize this phone, so I'm expecting a quick explanation of who you are and how you got this number." His voice was terse, professional, with an upper-crust New England accent.

"It's Quinn."

The line was silent for a few moments. "Well. This is a surprise, to be sure. A pleasant one, of course. I didn't expect to get a chance to thank you for…"

"Forget it." I didn't want to get into anything personal with him. Hollis March was the guy who introduced me to the world of forgery and knew everyone who was anyone in the game. He was also a deadly manipulator, a snake-in-the-grass who couldn't be trusted to share a bag of oxygen with a suffocating man.

"You could have made your life easier and your stay shorter if you'd named a few names in court. I'm grateful for that. They wouldn't have actually found me, but the problems and cost might have been considerable.

Ever the confident operator. "Forget it. We'll say you owe me a favor."

He was silent again. Hollis was like that, always composed, thinking a step ahead. "You wouldn't be calling, I'm guessing, unless you wanted to cash that favor in."

"It'll be the only call."

"I'm a little hurt by that. I was hoping we could make amends at some point. But I suppose…"

"We?" Then I caught myself and avoided getting into it with him. "Look… just skip it. Skip the dramatics and the bull. One favor. I need a name and address. First name is Polly, works in oils, lives in Jersey, great with old paper and canvass. Oh, and she's…"

"British, yes, I know. Polly Clark. She has an art store in Camden."

He even had the address, an older neighborhood in a town full of lousy old neighborhoods.

"If you need anything else…."

"Don't call me," I said, before hanging up.

The branch was only a few blocks from the Druid and I knew my father would be there. So I hoofed it over, the air cool and moist. Traffic seemed louder than normal, a jack hammer somewhere nearby doubtless further the futile Hell that was a typical Philly commute.

I felt dirty, having to call Hollis, having to use his experience. It wasn't exactly the way he'd used my talent; it was a damn sight better than that. But it still felt wrong.

At the Druid, my father had half a cold Straub on the

counter, the other half already in the glass. "So you called a source, and it happens he's the guy what brung you along as a criminal. This is different," he insisted. "You've got no cause to feel wrong tapping a confidential informant. We did it all the time."

"Yeah, but... this is a guy who used and manipulated me, Pa. It's like..."

"It's like calling a school bully years later for a job reference. You feel weakened by it."

"Humiliated. Yeah."

"Get over it." He swallowed the beer. "The fact of the matter is some of the godawfulest people you meet in this world will be the ones who can push your buttons, make you feel small." He turned and stared at me intensely. "But it's because it's all they've got. They have to go low, or they have no way to compete with you, not on fact or fancy. Use him for what you need, then don't t'ink another second of it."

"You wouldn't have needed to resort to..."

"Ptth!" He blew that idea away immediately. "Don't go buying any of the baloney you hear about my police days..."

"You're The Mighty Quinn. To some of these guys..."

"Well, the Mighty Quinn almost got his arse shot off on about a half-dozen occasions, each and everyone involving a stupid decision he made, in his so-called mighty wit and wisdom. Don't ever base what you want to do on me, Liam. You're good enough to forge your own path. Smart enough, too, even if you seem to forget to use the wee lump of grey between your ears every now and then."

And that's my old man, in a nutshell: he takes no credit, he offers no easy answers, he just tries to do what is right.

"It's hard."

"It always is. You remember that time when you was... ohhh, Lord, you must've been fifteen, at most. And you had a three-rounder, one of your first, set up with that boy from

Ocean City… the big lad. What was his name again?"

"Kieran Pryce. Nice kid."

"But an animal for his age in the ring. And he was two years older than you, already training with pros most of the time. You remember what happened in the third…"

"Yeah. He threw a little shoulder feint where he didn't even move the arm, he just flexed the muscle, and I slipped it a little, and he came around with the hard left hook, caught the side of my chin and jaw square, just about knocked my head off my shoulders."

"You were down!" Pa insisted. "Down and out, barely even conscious, flat on your back on the canvas."

"And you were in the corner, telling me to get up, telling me if I took it, if I lost like that – getting knocked out while wearing protective headgear – I'd be letting bums knock me out from then on in. You were like Burgess Meredith in Rocky, bickering away at me…"

He chuckled at that. "You should've heard your mother later than night for me trying to get you back into the fight. Oh, she tore one off my back something fierce."

"Yeah…" She was like that, claws out when it came to her boys. "Still… I got up, and I knocked poor Kieran on his ass three times in the third round… my bell ringing throughout."

"And that's why I don't worry." He drained the beer and set it down. "I'll get another, Marty…" He announced.

"Coming right up, Al," Marty said.

"I don't worry, because you always get up, Liam. You've never had the word quit in you. You won't this time. You'd never let the likes of Hollis March get the better of you."

Marty set the beer down. "Hey, let me get this one," I suggested.

Pa looked at me, puzzled. "Well, that was a given."

30.

By the time I'd gotten hold of Hollis March and nailed down Polly Clark's location, Walter had come through.

Pat Delaney was his partner's client, technically. But he'd been surprisingly eager to talk to me, Walter said, once he managed to get the conversation that far. Given our family history, I guess I wasn't that surprised. My father put Pat away more often than the good Scotch.

Most recently, he was a guest of the refined confines of State Correctional Institute Schuylkill, a concrete block behind barbed wire, two hours northwest of the city, near the town of Gordon, a main-street blip that last grew when the railroad was king and John Paul Getty was buying up land.

Deputy Warden McAndrew, a sullen, giant of a man with plain, square plastic eyeglass frames, met me at the steel mesh visitors' gate. He led me through the medium-security wing, past rows of cells with privacy doors, very un-Hollywood, to Pat's cellblock, which had its own meeting rooms adjacent to the cafeteria.

Before we entered, he said, "Well, I'll have a man right outside if you want any help. He's behind glass, so I don't imagine there could be a problem. But Delaney's apparently not fond of you in the slightest, Mr. Quinn. I expect you should prepare yourself for some colorful language."

"I'll keep it in mind, sir, thank you."

He opened the meeting room door. The guard nodded to him. "John…" he murmured. "Keep an ear out for Mr. Quinn and for any problems with the inmate, okay?" Then he gave me a similar nod. "Good luck to you, sir.'

Behind glass, Pat Delaney looked undersized, a balding, five-foot-something guy in a slightly large orange jumpsuit, the sleeves rolled up like he was trying to turn it into a choice. He reminded me of the stand-up comic, Jim Norton, only angrier and with -- judging from his neck's tree-trunk circumference -- prison muscles.

I took a seat and picked up the phone. "How're you doing Pat? How're they treating you?"

I know, it sounds pretty familiar, like I was going to kiss the guy's butt or something. But it's a standard prison thing, to inquire as to how the system has decided to beat a man down on that particular day.

He looked at the guard, then back at me, like he might venture an opinion in different company. Instead, he said, "What do you want, Quinn? I'm curious, because Walter dropped all sorts of comments about it being about me... but not much else. Like he was teasing information to get me to play along, or something. I really ought to bust him in the mouth the next time I see him."

"Charming. Is that charm why Polly is so into you? Or does she just have abuse issues?"

His expression remained glib and unchanging. "Who?"

"Uh huh. Whatever you've got her up to with that Dufresne..."

"Like I said, I never heard of this person."

"Then... if I look at your visitor lists, I won't see her name front and center."

He blew it off. "Ptth! Like I give a crap! Go ahead, look all you want."

Which was good... because I'd kept my little recorder running, and I wanted his permission to look at personal information on the record for when I asked McArthur. "Whatever you're up to, your old crew isn't too happy."

"What do I care? I'm stuck in here for a few years yet,

Quinn. I'm out of business. So Teddy gets a little riled up…"

"I didn't say it was Teddy, and you've worked with…what, a half-dozen guys at least…"

He shrugged his shoulders. "Most recent. I was taking a stab at it. I heard he drowned."

"Not so much. In fact, I think he believes he has a shot at the middleweight title or something."

"Uh huh." He studied me. "Did you knock him on his ass? I remember you, kid. I was in school with your brother, Andy? Did you know that? That was before your old man started busting my balls every chance he got."

"By 'busting your balls' I assume you mean 'enforcing the law as a police officer'."

"Same difference. Not surprised you dealt with Teddy, though, if you're not lying about that. You were a Hell of a fighter, kid. I won a few bucks on you. Either way, you've got a set the size of a Buick, showing up here and expecting to get my help."

"Nah… I just figured you haven't done the math yet," I said. "If I know you're neck deep in this, so does the guy you stole the painting from in the first place: Vincent Terrasini."

He looked nonplussed. Whatever else he qualified as, Pat was an expert at acting innocent. "So? That supposed to worry me? Did you think you'd come up here, get me shaking in my boots at the octogenarian?"

"What about your former cellmate… the little guy…"

"Kevin Walsh. What about him."

"He's not worried? Because everyone and his brother already has it figure as him and his friend who hit the gallery. You think Vin's going to play nice with him? Or the guys in your old crew?"

He turned his head away real quick to hide his reaction; I knew that got to him, at least a little. But he wasn't giving anything away. "He's a big boy, so is Charlie. They can take care of themselves. You, on the other hand, seem to forget the other aspect to how many people I know on the outside."

"Yeah? You going to sick your dogs on me, Pat? I'm shaking."

He smiled and nodded a few times. Then he got up and turned to leave. He looked back once, just long enough to give me the finger.

31.

Polly Clark's shop was in a small, aging strip mall, next to a bakery that had grease and dirt caked onto the windowpanes and looked like it hadn't opened since the Nixon administration. The cracks in the parking lot asphalt were being filled in by grass, white paint peeling off the posts that fronted the handful of parking spaces.

Polly was behind a throwing wheel against the front wall when I walked in, up to her elbows in muddy, wet clay. The place was chaotic, with tables covering at least half the floorspace in no discernable pattern, works stacked on some, others still on easels. "Hi!" she said. "I'll be right with you."

"No rush," I said. "Just browsing."

I walked along parallel to the wall, admiring a series of oils. Her work was eclectic, impersonal, like someone trying to prove a point with flash over substance. I couldn't get any unifying theme between them, anything uniquely hers. Some featured thick strokes that left swirling waves of texture clumped above the surface; others were so delicate and fine, it was difficult to tell which medium had been used.

It was easy to see why she'd been a good forger. It was a hodgepodge of some of the most-taught approaches to putting oil on canvas. But none were done in anything resembling expert technique. On occasion, this helped her, as she mirrored the naïve strokes of natural talent without even meaning to do so.

"Do you see anything you like?" she said, wiping her hands and forearms off with a damp cloth and then drying them on a towel. She walked over and stood next to me when I reached the largest.

"Good eye," she said, her British accent still intact after

being in Philly and Camden for several years. "That's one of my favorites. I turned down five thousand pounds for it on my last trip to London."

I looked around the place; the room was cruddy, and dusty, a labor of love long gone wrong, abandoned by the public. I doubted there was toilet paper in the bathroom, let alone five thousand worth of anything on display.

"Really? Five thousand? Because to me, it's derivative of a Manet, to the point where you even seem to have adopted some of his brush stroke."

Her face hardened. "You fuzz?"

"Excuse me?"

"No one comes in my store talking about technique like that unless they're someone I already know... or they're a cop looking to hassle me. And I don't know you, which leaves ..."

"I'm a private insurance investigator. And a former art student."

"Yeah? Well maybe you should bugger off, then. I don't have to talk to you."

That was irritating. "You don't even know why I'm here."

"I don't want to know," she said. "Can't be anything good."

"Really? A guy showed up at my store asking questions, I'd want to know why."

"So... you're curious. Again: why should I care?"

I didn't have many cards to play. If she was involved, perhaps fear would shake something loose. "Oh, I don't know.... maybe because Vin the Shin is after the same answers I am. If I was in your boat, and I was maybe just a little involved, I'd want to take advantage of any opportunity presented to extricate myself."

That shut her up as she thought about things. "I know the name. But I don't know him and I don't have nothing to do with him."

It came out as "dunavnuffink to dowivim."

She was going to play dumb, which was a shame. "Polly, who do you think gave me you? He's already on to you, whatever you and Pat Delaney are up to."

Clark laughed at that one. "Really? You think I'm still with that waste of space? You really are barking up the wrong tree, mate. I mean, yeah, I did a job for Terrasini once. But that was two years ago, and I never even met the man."

"And Pat? Have you seen him since? If you've been visiting him in jail, I'm going to find out."

She sneered. "I told you, I haven't talked to him since he went away. He was a real tough guy, you know?"

I wasn't straight on the implication. That he was knocking her around? In the Delaney household that was practically a given.

"So, are you scared of him? Is that it?"

She laughed at that, too. "He's inside. What have I got to be scared of?"

"You tell me."

She stared at me silently for a minute, her mouth a grim line. "Yeah, all right, I'm scared of him. You happy? But I haven't seen him, and we're not together."

"Have you heard from him at all? Or about him, from any of his old friends? Kevin Walsh maybe?"

"I don't have to talk to you, arsehole! Besides, Pat isn't the kind who's real sentimental about his friendships. Look, are you going to leave me alone? Because I don't have to talk to no one without a lawyer."

"Like I said, Vin the Shin might be interested in all of this."

"Yeah, well… over to you." She turned away, her arms crossed defiantly, like an angry kid making a point.

"Hey… you know, here's another idea: you may be so

damaged that you think you're too small-fry for Vincent Terrasini to care about. But maybe Pat's buddies from the armored car heist would want to know what you've been up to, as well. How do you think that would go, there, Pol?"

She turned to look at me quickly, betraying her curiosity.

"That get your attention?" I was maybe a bit glib about it, if I'm being straight with youse.

She said, "You don't read the papers much, do you?"

"What, the bit about them both disappearing in the river? Yeah… I don't put too much stock in that."

"No?"

"Well, considering I went part of a round with Teddy Armas the other night, and he went down real solid when I hit him, I have a hard time believing he was a ghost. A ghost of the 'Golden Gloves' champ he allegedly used to be. That, I believe."

Her face deadpanned again. "Yeah, I'm supposed to buy that, am I? That a pretty boy like you knocked out Teddy? That you even met him?"

I studied her. She was in her mid-twenties, much younger than Pat, pretty, but overweight and out of shape, lines around her eyes betraying tensions and problems that weren't supposed to wear down people her age.

"But you do believe me, don't you Polly? Because if you didn't already know they made it out of the river, you'd have been shocked when I suggested they did. Or worried."

"Yeah?"

"Yeah. And you'd have been shocked or worried because you and Pat are up to something. I've got to figure if I'm looking for you, and they're looking for me? Well, at the end of that line somewhere is the money missing from that armored car heist. If they made it out, the money might have, too."

She wasn't going to tell me jack. "I think you should get

out of my store. You're not a cop and I don't have to talk to you. Go on, get out!"

She was practically shoving me towards the front door, which was probably fortunate timing on her part: it was the same exact moment Teddy Armas and his two accomplices decided to come in through the back door.

Teddy was already pulling a nine-millimeter.

32.

I grabbed Polly by the wrist and pulled her towards the main door. "We need to be leaving."

"Hey!" Teddy Armas yelled, pulling back the slide on his pistol.

I shoved the door open and sprinted outside. She ran after me, half trying to keep stride, half trying to pull away. We crossed the small parking lot to my car. "Get in!" I yelled.

She stood there, torn. Then Teddy and the boys burst through the front doors.

"We're out of time, they're armed, get in," I said, leaning over the passenger seat to talk to her through the Firebird's open window.

Regardless of what she thought of me, the young crook wasn't stupid. She climbed in and I hit the gas, just in time for a bullet to shatter the back windshield.

Dammit.

I worked for an insurance agency ... and had no glass coverage.

But it's not like anyone reminded me about that, right?

We peeled out of the lot, their green sedan squealing out about two hundred yards behind us. I downshifted and took us around the first corner on a freewheeling roll, asphalt blackened by haste and desperation. The sedan flew around right after us, fishtailing, almost rolling onto two tires... but hanging in there.

On the wide MLK Boulevard I gunned the Firebird's big engine, running us in and out of the other traffic. The sedan was having trouble keeping pace now, its handling insufficient to the task, the car's frame bouncing off other cars, drivers swerving, more back axles fishtailing wildly. Polly cringed reflexively as she heard the cars begin to careen into one another, the crunch, thud and crash of breaking glass.

Me? I wasn't even looking back. As we approached the cross street at Haddon, it was obvious the mess behind us was at least going to slow them down. The light was already yellow, and we were still thirty yards away. We blew into the intersection with me frantically braking and shifting, the engine howling in protest as the car wound down through the gears and I pulled us hard to the left, just as the rest of the traffic flow shifted direction.

The sedan had gotten around the tangle behind us, but hadn't made the light, and the large concrete divide made catching up impossible.

I waited until we found a quiet side street then pulled the car over. "Okay, so you're absolutely sure you haven't talked to Patrick Delaney in the last few weeks?"

She shot me a cold, defensive look, but said nothing.

I added, "Because that sure as hell looked like Teddy Armas and the rest of Pat's old gang."

Still she said nothing, instead crossing her arms at her midsection, defensively. "I'm as surprised as you are those guys are still around," she said, with all the fervent conviction of a crook who couldn't think up a clever lie on the spot.

"Want to know what I think, Polly?"

"I'm sure you're going to tell me."

She was still defiant, but nervous, maybe even a little scared.

"I think your boy Pat recovered the money. And they think you've got a handle on it. So maybe they stole that forgery because it gives them something on you. Or maybe they know it means something to you."

She half-smiled, a true poker 'tell.' I was wrong, and she knew it. And I had no authority to keep grilling her. She knew that, too.

"They said on the news they got away with a ton of

cash," she said.

"So?"

"So... if I had that kind of money, do you think I'd still be living in Camden and working in a strip mall?"

"I don't know what you'd do, Polly."

"No? Well then I'll tell you: I'd bugger off back across the ocean to my own country, where men are still at least a little bit dependable."

Sure, that was Polly Clark. Ms. Dependable herself. "You don't have anything to say about that little chase just now?"

"You going to let me out of your car now, or is this a kidnapping?"

"There's nothing stopping you."

She smiled gracefully ... and then she spat in my face.

"Screw you."

She slammed the door when she climbed out. I hate it when people slam my car doors. I wiped the spit off and watched her go around the corner of the alley and disappear.

As I drove home, there was no doubt in my mind she was lying; she knew where the heist money was stashed, or at the very least Pat's old gang thought she did. There wasn't much point in them shaking her down otherwise – and I had a hard time seeing Teddy Armas being into arts and crafts.

33.

After I got back into Philly, I grabbed a roast beef bagel and a coffee to take home with me then headed back to the loft. When I got up to my floor, Ricky had his door open a crack again... but this time was peeking through it and, after scoping me out, closed it quickly as if not wanting to be seen.

I thought about going over and knocking, confronting the issue head on. A few months earlier, when I'd moved in, Ricky was part of the welcome wagon, making sure I got to know everybody in the building. He was engaging and self-confident.

Despite having had some success prior to my big letdown, self-confidence had never really been my closest of friends. I did a good job of faking it when necessary, but the guy inside wasn't socially graceful. If you grew up in Fishtown in the Eighties, you had to have a hard shell. So when it came to telling people I was sorry, to putting humility out there for judgment and taking my chances...

I was going to have to talk to him at some point about it. He didn't deserve the stress he'd had to endure, thanks to Vin the Shin's goons, and that was my fault for bringing them there in the first place. His reaction at the door suggested maybe he felt the same way.

For now, I contented myself to finally catch up on the day's news, to down my bagel and to try to relax for a night with a good book.

I love to read. Before prison, I wasn't the biggest reader. It wasn't that I didn't enjoy a good piece of fiction, I just never had the time, it seemed.

But in prison you've got all sorts of time – nothing but, as a wise man once said. So, I'd worked myself into the habit of making sure I took at least a few hours every day to read something new.

One paragraph in, my phone rang.

"Liam?"

It was Alison Pace.

"Look, I was just in the neighborhood and I thought I'd stop around and see what kind of progress you were making," she said with the same warm, charming tone that had been on display the first time we'd talked.

"You're downstairs?"

"Uh-huh."

"It's 3B. I'll buzz you in," I said.

About a minute later she knocked on the door. When I opened it, she looked stunning, in a sheer grey dinner gown, at once both formal and provocative, elegantly cut but with a plunging neckline that flattered her cleavage. Her hair was held up and the jewelry looked like it could have paid for my loft with relative ease.

"I'm sorry," she said. "I should have called before..."

"No. No, it's okay," I said. "I'm never really off the clock. Please..." I motioned for her to come in and she walked past me, the back of the dress slit open down to the base of her spine, accentuating her tanned skin.

"I was at a charity event down the street. I just wanted to thank you for taking this all so seriously," she said, as I pointed to the opposite couch. "I understand from John that you've made a number of inquiries."

"It's nothing – makes my job a lot easier if I know where everyone stands," I said. "Would you like a glass of wine?"

She nodded. "Please."

I moved to the sideboard and poured us each a healthy dose. She downed hers in two swallows, before I'd even sat back down. "Another?" I said, giving her a squint.

"Thanks," she said, accepting it gratefully.

"Why am I guessing the stress of all of this is wearing on you a bit?"

She nodded. "I think Leo and I are going to break up. It's just... I don't know... 'uninteresting' now? I'm not sure we even got as far as supportive. Getting engaged was... way premature."

"That's difficult."

Alison nodded, pushing back her hair with an air of reflex tension. "It's not even the worst of it. I have to worry about my job, too. It's... well, we were already having financial troubles before the robbery even happened. I mean, I don't know if you know but..."

"I talked to John at length. His problems aren't a big secret."

"So you know about Carl and Dennis Hecht?"

"Dennis?"

"Carl's brother and business advisor. Cold guy."

"So... peas from the same rotten pod?"

She took a sip of wine and sort of drifted off a little, gazing spacily over its brim. "Sort of, yeah."

Then she looked over the brim at me, fixing me with her dark eyes. "Doesn't look like you're sharing this place. You're single?"

I nodded, but didn't say anything, watching the dimmed overhead light glint off her lipstick as she took a sip. I couldn't help but think that that was one lucky glass.

She got up and walked over to the window, holding her drink close, staring out at the city lights. "I just need to forget about all this whole mess, you know? Even if it's just for a few hours."

I joined her and watched the glow, far into the distance. "It's always dazzling at night, the lights and motion, the constant blur of activity, fully involved but out of reach... behind glass."

She turned, close to me and looked up into my eyes. I could feel the warmth of her close to me. "Quinn..." she said, moving closer.

I shook my head gently and put a finger to her lips. "Shhh.... You're a client, I'm working on your case, and you're my best friend's friend."

Alison looked wistful. "So... nothing?"

"No. Highly flattered, and you sure don't make saying no easy, but... bad timing."

She looked back down at the lights, watching Philadelphia's night stretch on, the ribbon of vehicles heading down 21st Street. "Isn't that always the way?" she said. She finished her glass of wine. "I should go."

"No rush."

"You're being very nice, but..."

"No, I mean it. Last of the genuine nice guys."

"You're cute as hell, you know that?"

I didn't, but she'd had a couple of glasses of wine, so I took the compliment. "Thank you."

"I don't know why Nora doesn't talk about you more," she said.

Ouch.

I said, "Well, we've known each other a long time. We don't really have any secrets."

"But you two...?"

"Nope." I bit my lip.

"She doesn't know what she's missing."

Oh... I was pretty sure she did. "Again, flattery is appreciated, but will get you nowhere."

She downed the rest of her glass. "Drink up, and we'll see in a couple of hours," she said.

And so she stayed for one more glass, and one more, and we talked until about half past midnight, eventually revisiting the sleeping arrangements: after way too many glasses of wine for her to risk driving, she took the bed, and I took the couch.

In no time, I was dreaming of forgeries that were more valuable than the real thing, my tired brain trying to figure out what that had to do with an armored-car load of money.

I had a few hours the next day before meeting everyone at the Druid, so I hooked up with DeShawn Ellis at a cafe in Center City.

He was waiting for me in one of the wood panel booths, looking awkward. My guess was he didn't get out of West Philly much, except to work.

"Hey Mr. Quinn," he said. "My moms told me you'd found me another job."

"Yeah, something away from David Mince. Are you okay with that?"

He shrugged. "Not really. I mean, I'm glad for what you did and all. But I like to solve my own problems. I know David thinks I'm real slow..."

"David's an idiot disguised as someone shrewd," I said. "I mean, he may have a certain animal survival instinct, but I wouldn't expect him to take the smart road most of the time. He's more of a 'look for the shortcut, no matter how it hurts others' kind of guy."

The waitress came over with a pair of plastic-laminated menus. "You fellas hungry? Got a special today on the veal chop for lunch."

"Just coffee for me," I said. "You want a soda or something?"

The kid nodded. "I'll get a ..." He looked hesitantly at me, like I might react badly, "... a vanilla milkshake?"

The waitress smiled. "I'll throw an extra scoop in there for ya, use that mixing cup proper."

"See, you ask nicely and sometimes..." I began to say.

"I learned early not to speak up, Mr. Quinn. If you think too much and talk to much..."

"Yeah, I get that," I said. "I was a weird kid, believe me, at least as far as the other kids were concerned. Fortunately, life is much more than childhood."

Our other guest entered the diner and made his way over to our table. "Liam," Clinton Dufresne said. "I suppose this is the young man you were telling me about..."

"DeShawn, this is my friend Clinton..."

DeShawn snapped to his feet, eyes wide. "I know who you are. I saw your picture in the newspaper. You famous..."

Clinton held out a fist and the boy bumped it. "Clinton Dufresne. And you must be..."

"DeShawn, sir. DeShawn Ellis. My mama is going to be real excited that I met you."

"Well that's real nice to hear, my brother, thank you! Thank you for the recognition."

"She said you're going to run for city council."

I gave Clinton a quizzical look. "Is that true? I hadn't heard that."

He shot me a sly glance back. "It's possible, Liam, just possible, that you don't travel in the right social circles to hear absolutely everything."

Ouch. DeShawn pointed at my face. "See... yeah! If you blush like a Stop sign chances are you don't know what's going on in my neighborhood."

"So it's true?" I asked.

"I'm giving it serious consideration, sure," Clinton said. "People in the community keep asking, expecting me to take the next career steps, make it a leadership role to take advantage of my exposure."

"You sound like maybe they're demanding it but you're not so sure."

"I wouldn't go that far," he replied. "I like the idea plenty. I just like to think things through, is all. Speaking of which, did you get anywhere on the whole picture switch?"

"Maybe. Let's say the picture wasn't what was important. Maybe there's a message in the painting itself, the forgery I mean. Or maybe there's something secreted in the frame."

"Like a password," DeShawn said.

"Or a key," Clinton said. "They wouldn't have been able to deposit the stolen money anywhere. They'd need to wash it as soon as they recovered it, maybe lose it at a series of casinos, buying and then cashing in chips."

I got his drift. "So they needed a place to stash it that was public and open, that wouldn't be closely monitored and could be accessed at any time..."

In a city of more than two million people, that was about as vague as it got. Clinton could tell from the look on my face that I knew how big the haystack was, and how small the needle."

"You need to talk to your old man and his cop buddies," he suggested. "IF anyone's going to narrow it down, it's the people who deal with forgers and thieves on the regular. And you, young blood..."he said to DeShawn. "I hear Liam's found you a new job and you're planning on going to college."

The boy nodded. "But I'm a year behind on account of my autism," he said. "I'm not stupid. I just think things through differently..."

Clinton smiled warmly, gently. "I know. Liam and me, we were both seen as 'different' when we were young. He was a boxer and I was painting already. Tell me, D, you have a class you're real good at, maybe ahead of everyone else?"

DeShawn nodded vigorously. "Math. Yeah... I don't do so good at history and English and the hard ones. But math is real easy for me."

"Your school know that?"

He shrugged. "They think I'm retarded or something?"

"Delayed, son, delayed. Don't use the 'r' word no more, okay? Hurts kids that are..." He caught himself almost using the wrong word. "Delayed. Okay?"

"Yeah. Yeah, sure, I get that."

"Maybe I could have a word with them, see if they can revisit their efforts on you finishing a little earlier and then look at some areas where your math skills might fit, like computer science or engineering, physics..."

DeShawn's eyes widened. "Really? You think I could do that stuff?"

Clinton shrugged. "I think you'll amaze everybody with what you can do. Either way, I figure it's worth trying, right?"

The kid smiled at that, a big, broad, beaming smile, the kind I hadn't seen on his young mug until then. And that felt pretty damn good.

34.

AT THE DRUID, THEY HAD an Irish band playing on the patio – anything to get the younger guys in on a Monday night.

It wasn't working so well. The same regular crew of wide-bodied old ex-cops were flattening the same old bar stools. Davy had come out, though – right from work – and was chatting animatedly with Pa, my brother's crew-cut red hair a contrast to our father's silvery locks, and his frame many, many donuts short of retirement.

I couldn't hear what they were arguing about until I'd pushed the folks milling around and managed to get closer.

"Your brother, bless his foolish heart, thinks most people would feel safer and be happier if they had a gun in the house," said Pa.

Davy gave me a quick glance but didn't say hello, instead turning back to our dad. "In Switzerland, it's the law. And that's one of the most peaceful countries on Earth."

Dad shook his head. "That's fine if you're already doing okay, if you're a secure person with a normal life. And most of those guns in Switzerland are long rifles, for purposes of a national militia – you know, like the Second Amendment? But you'd put a gun in every house in West Philly?"

On dad's other side, former traffic cops Melvin Guest and Mike Barber had been listening in, and Melvin laughed at dad's suggestion. "You put a gun in every household in West Philly, you end up with a lot of dumb dead dude. Now, I know you're arguing that's a bad thing, Al…"

Davy was about to argue back, but I interjected. "It's true. It's not the gun, it's the circumstance that causes someone to use it that's important. The poorer and more desperate they are, the more often they use guns the wrong way. So it matters who has access, and when."

My brother looked at me cynically. "Yeah? I call bull."

"Then explain why they have open carry laws for handguns in both Maine and Arizona, but only Arizona has serious gun crime."

Davy squinted, trying to figure out the dichotomy. "Yeah? One has millions of people and a border a hundred miles away, the other doesn't. What do you know anyway? You spend too much time talking to your criminal buddies."

"He's got a point there," Mike Barber chimed in.

Really? My criminal buddies? "I'll tell you what, Davy, they may be a bunch of criminals but at least they're not dumb enough to think we should give every household a gun. This isn't Switzerland. There's too much income disparity and unhappiness in America. Our gun death rate is more than twice the nearest other developed nation even when you take out the suicides that account for..."

"Nonsense!" Davy insisted. "They still kill themselves in those countries, they just use other methods, which is why Sweden – which everyone seems to want to hold up as what America should be like – has a higher suicide rate than we do."

My father had made up his mind a long time ago. He was never a firearms fan, even when he saw the need. So even when Davy made a point he sort of agreed with, he couldn't give. "I don't know about that, son... I just know there's so many goddamn guns in this country..."

Melvin was nodding, but Davy seemed almost taken aback. "I can't believe what I'm hearing. You guys agree with this moral relativity, this 'a civil right is always bad if someone else can't handle it" bull?" He slugged back the last of his beer and got up to leave. "You got to come where I drink and ruin life here too, right?"

I sighed and tilted my head back reflexively in a show of frustration. "Davy, come on. I'm not even completely disagreeing with you. I just think it's impossible to ignore the statistics, the weekly school shootings…"

"Don't you 'come on' me," he said, hat under his arm as always when off duty. "You've done some real stupid things in the last few years, but everyone else ends up paying for your damage," he said. "Please… don't act like you have an answer to all of our problems. 'No guns'. What a bunch of garbage…"

Mike jerked a thumb in Davy's direction. "I'm inclined to agree with the kid. Lot harder to get shot if you shoot the guy first."

"That's you," I suggested. "Your little brother Frank, who last I checked was still doing a dime at CFCF, would pull the trigger before you crossed the street from your car to the stoop. He wouldn't wait to find out if you were a problem… or selling encyclopedias."

Davy turned quickly and shot me a hard look. "You should stay out of this. You're a criminal. You don't get the choice, remember? You blew your right to carry. Don't try and screw it up for everyone else!"

"Davy…."

He held up a hand. "Ah! Forget about it. I'm out of here." And then he strode out of the room, going through the balcony door so he could stop and light a quick smoke on the "patio."

I guess Pa saw the hurt look on my face, because he put a reassuring hand on my shoulder. "I know you want your brother to accept you again. But don't let that get you thinking he's always right, and you're always wrong. 'Cause it ain't so. Or vice-versa for that matter."

Melvin harrumphed once indignantly. "Always? Liam, your brother's arguments… he's a good kid, Davy, but he couldn't win a debate over whether water was wet if he fell out of a boat."

Dad took a little intake of breath at that, about to snap at him for haranguing his boy. But he caught himself and didn't argue. "He ain't my brightest." He glanced at me sideways. "Then again, my brightest ain't so bright neither, judging on recent history. 'Bright' and 'smart' are often not the same damn thing."

He had that right. I told him about the chase and the forger, and Vin the Shin. Terrasini's involvement seemed to worry Pa to no end.

"You stay away from those guys, you hear? The amount of trouble you've been in already, any of our boys finds out you're talking to Vin the Shin, they'll make you as dirty in a second."

"I didn't exactly have an option, Pa. He scooped me off the middle of the street. Besides, he's got reasons for needing this case solved himself."

I went through the story of the Dufresne theft, the forgery and the robbery at Vin the Shin's condo.

Pa rolled his eyes Heavenward. "You just can't avoid trouble, even when you're doing the right thing."

Melvin hadn't seen me in years. "You still boxing, Liam? I remember that fight you had with Artie Clooney, when you was about fifteen or sixteen. That seven-punch combo that put him down was something else."

Most people wouldn't have believed it, but that combo was a legit sequence shown me by my manager at the time. It was also the past, and it was done. "Nah, just a working stiff now, Mr. Guest."

My dad muttered under his breath, then finished the short glass of whisky he'd ordered between beers. "You keep working for Vin the Shin, you'll be a real stiff," he said.

"I just have to resolve this case, Pa; then I'll never see

the guy again."

"So… what's taking so long?"

"Pieces. Lots of pieces. But I met this guy, this architect. Clinton Dufresne. He sort of got my head straight on some things. Like maybe the key to this thing is an actual key. They had to stash the money somewhere."

I should note that my father knew damn well as a cop that a blind robbery like this could take months or years to solve, if ever. I probably had a month or two at most before the company started talking about write-downs, starting with my commission.

Mike said, "You should keep tabs on the girlfriend. No doubt she's lying. Ten'll get you one it's a combination locker at the airport or a lockbox at a storage depot. Something publicly easily accessible, innocuous, never really checked. And you're wrong about guns, Liam. They're just tools. Now, the person using them, may, unfortunately, also be a tool. But Canadians have, per household, as many guns as Americans, and yet their death rate is a fraction. So… it's not the guns. It's the people using them. Maybe what we have is a lot of poor, angry, desperate and stupid people. Maybe that's the problem to address, not three hundred years of civil engineering that keeps us alive."

I sighed. "Fine. I don't want to argue it anymore, Mike. You went sort of meta on me there, and yeah, there is a bigger picture."

Dad got us back on track. "Follow the money, Liam. Pat Delaney's on the inside for four more years. But the money is on the outside and so is she, and his former crew has it in for her. Doesn't take a mathematician. Follow the girl, eventually she'll lead you to the money, or she'll lead you to the former cellmate, Kevin Walsh. My money's on him as your lead shotgun robber.

They had a point, although it didn't explain why they

needed that copy of the Dufresne so badly. Plus, I've done a few stakeouts in the past, and they're the worst, hours of just sitting there with nothing to do but read and watch and, typically, record dead air.

Pa saw my hangdog look. "Hey, that's why you should have been a cop," he said. "When you got a partner, it's a lot easier to kill time: one guy can watch while the other takes a nap, for instance. And even if you don't find nothing, you still get a paycheck at the end of the month. Assuming the payroll computer is working."

That gave me an idea. I didn't have a partner, but I had a guy who owed me big time, and that was going to have to do.

35.

Danny Saint was still working the Washington Park area but had branched out from Three-Card Monte to hosting a dice game.

Hosting dice is smart, from a criminal perspective. The odds are so thoroughly against the player – it ain't roulette bad, but it's up there – that the house never does too badly. Of course, the easier the money, the more heat you got from other operators.

If you were a smooth enough roller, you could flop out the dice for an identical pair weighted to roll snake eyes most of the time. Then there was no doubting who was going home happy.

The dice game was behind a Wawa store just off the park's south side. Players were rolling up against the back wall, trying to match their earlier rolls or get a natural seven or eleven. Judging by the thatch of bills in Danny's hand, the house was even more crooked than usual.

I walked up behind him quietly. "You know, for a guy whose last name is Saint, you sure do break the rules a whole lot."

He muttered under his breath. "Ixnay on the eating-chay," he said. "I got a nice old grandma in a home to support."

It's true, although nice was a stretch. Danny's grandma was ninety-four and still tough as nails. She'd laughed when Danny had told her he'd just gotten out of jail again and asked why he was hanging out "with some bastard Mick from Fishtown." Then she'd punched him in the shoulder.

I kept my voice equally low. "Yeah? Well how do you think the grandmothers of all these fine gentlemen would feel if they knew you were cheating their grandbabies with your crooked dice?"

Danny held up both hands promptly and spoke loudly. "Gentlemen! Last roll! Due to exigent circumstances I must avail myself of, uh…elsewhere."

The four guys rolling whined and complained… but all four put most of their roll down on the final pass.

Danny took them clean one more time, then picked up his dice and quickly switched them out for the good ones. He took a half-step back from where he'd been standing, but was challenged by the roller, a young African-American guy with a neatly trimmed beard. "Man, you got almost every roll in the last ten minutes," he said. "Lemme see them dice."

It could have gotten ugly quickly, but Danny's switch had been perfect. He handed the pair to the roller, who tried them a few times. Three of the four rolls were naturals, seven or 11.

"Damn," said the man.

His friends laughed at him. They picked themselves up and dusted off to leave, and I led Danny to the edge of the lot.

"All right," he said. "What's so important you got to cut off that sort of action?"

I filled him in. "Now Vin the Shin's expecting results."

His eyes widened and he shook a finger at me. "Oh no. You're not dragging me into that kind of business. No mobbed up guys, no stand up guys, no wise guys. Not today, not this week, not ever."

"Look, all I need you to do is stake out a woman, keep tabs on her for a few days, see if she does anything funny."

"You mean funny like 'It's funny how Liam Quinn just ruined my dice game and probably cost me a grand' funny?"

I smiled. "Exactly."

"Ever occur to you that I got better things…"

"No."

"That kind of consideration? That right there is why we're so tight," Danny said.

"You do remember me protecting your butt inside the pen? I mean, those Aryan guys thought you were one purdy lil' thang."

Danny was never a tough guy. He got his ass kicked more than once on a long road trip with his ball club because he had choice words about another player's wife. Or slept with another player's wife and/or sister. His parents were crooks who reappeared when his baseball career began to take off, having given him up to a series of foster homes before then, the kind of places where the children left filled with nightmares or even more horrifically, real memories.

To people who knew him he was loyal and cheerful and charming and, usually, pretty honest. Everyone else fell into the general category of 'hunt or be hunted. I'm not going to pretend I liked it or that we spent a lot of time together, as a result. We knew where we stood with each other. He was grateful, I had a grudging respect for his ability to survive a hard life, even if I couldn't agree with how he'd accomplished it.

He sucked on his tongue for a moment, grumpily. "Never going to let me live prison down, are you?"

I nodded. "Never. But now I need your help. So just think of it as positive affirmation."

"Staking out a forger as 'positive affirmation.' You're one of a kind, Quinn," he said.

"And thank goodness it's true," I said.

When he'd gotten out of the pen, Danny had tried to go straight. He'd been a golf pro, something he intended to go back to, he promised. He'd been assistant manager of a fast food restaurant, something he vowed never to go back to, and that he'd rather be in prison. He'd worked odd jobs at a radio station, and for a local businessman with shady connections.

In each case, he'd been honest about his time inside and put it on his resume. In each case, they'd hired him without really looking closely at it. And in each case, they'd later found out and fired him regardless of the great job he'd been doing, the effort he'd made to go straight for really the first time outside of his baseball career.

So while I didn't agree with what he did, I was neither surprised that he did nor shocked that he felt very little for his victims. Up until we became friends, I'm not sure anyone showed even a moment of care and love for Danny Saint.

36.

At Philly Mutual's Center City building, Ramon was slurping Japanese noodles out of a Styrofoam cup.

"Hey, kid," he said when I walked into his office. "Some of my buddies from the department say you were talking about Vin the Shin Terrasini down at the Druid."

The cop grapevine traveled fast. "He's got an interest," I said, trying to keep things as vague as possible. "But don't worry, he didn't rob the place."

"If you know that, then you must have some idea who did," he said.

"Sort of, yeah. There are still a couple of pieces I haven't figured out yet."

"Are we going to take a bath on this one, or what?"

"Don't know yet. Depends on whether whoever took the painting has sold it yet. Maybe we can get it back still."

"Whoever? I thought you just said you..."

"I said 'sort of.' Can't be sure yet."

"Walk with me," he said. We headed back out into the main part of the office, where everyone was working, and over to the coffee maker, where Ramon poured himself a small cup. He'd taken one sip when I heard Nora's voice behind me.

"You're actually showing up at work? Wonders never cease."

I couldn't help but smile whenever I saw her, at least a little.

Her father interjected. "Quinn says he's going to recover that Vermeer, save the company a bundle."

Nora's eyes narrowed. "And a good piece of change for you, I imagine?"

"Have to figure. I don't know what they're pegging it at

yet...."

Ramon said, "They figure replacement value about ten mill right now, I hear."

"So that's just over two hundred and fifty grand for you, if I remember the percentages right," said Nora. "You buying dinner? A restaurant, maybe?"

Ramon's assistant walked over and interrupted. "That reminds me, Liam," she said. "You had a call. She said she lost your number, but she had a great time the other night and you should give her a ring back. Name was Alison something.... I got her number on a sticky on my desk somewhere..."

I cringed, waiting for a smart-ass comment from someone. Unfortunately, it was Nora. "Ooh, Liam," she said. "Alison!" She nodded approvingly after she said it. "You are a naughty boy."

I held up both hands. "Hey, she's a client. I don't get involved with clients," I said.

"Keep it that way," Ramon said as he walked back to his office.

Nora turned back to me. "What...?"

"She's a client," I said. "Besides, shouldn't you be a little more upset that neither of us cleared anything with you first? She's your friend."

That puzzled her and she paused. "Since when did you worry about what I think?"

My eyebrows shot up faster than a helium balloon. "You're kidding, right? I mean, geez, I always try to think of you first."

Nora squinted at me. Or, maybe if I'm being honest it was more of a frown.

"You're infuriating sometimes, you know that? I get you all figured out, and ...."

And there you have it. She's a riddle wrapped in an

enigma put through a KGB cypher machine or something. Women: you can't figure them out, you can't stop trying to figure them out. I know I can be a meathead sometimes, but trying to figure out what was eating Nora sometimes was just baffling. We'd be having the best time, and I'd say something completely innocuous, and on come the dramatics. What was I missing, exactly? I know my judgment has never been that sound, or I wouldn't have wound up in the joint for four years. But she sure was odd sometimes.

She didn't get a chance to finish the sentence before Ramon walked back into the room and interrupted. "Hey Liam: you better get your rubber boots on. I just got a call from my friend in robbery. He says they pulled two stiffs out of the river this morning... and one of them was Pat Delaney's old cellmate."

I made my apologies to Nora for needing to get back to work and pointed the Beast in the direction of Old City.

They still had yellow-and-black tape up around the scene a half-mile south of the Ben Franklin Bridge, in Dickinson Narrows. It was a trendy neighborhood of shops and restaurants, a tiny strip by the waterfront in an area of town that once hosted iron works and the Russian Jewish population of the city.

There were tracks in the muddy bank, where they'd used a four-wheel drive vehicle to help haul corpses on sleds up the steep slope. A cruiser was parked nearby and I knocked on the driver-side window, where a young officer was sitting drinking coffee.

"Yeah?"

Ever friendly, Philly's finest.

"Hey. Name's Quinn, insurance investigator. They ID

those two floaters from this morning?"

He looked up at me annoyed. "I can't tell you that, you know that. You've got to contact communications or the precinct staff sergeant for that crap."

I rolled my eyes. "Look, my dad's a retired member, my brother's on shift in the 35th, and it's all over already that one of the guys was Pat Delaney's cellmate."

He shrugged. "Don't know the players. Wouldn't know about that. Sorry. You talk to robbery yet?"

I shook my head. He looked on his multi-display terminal for a moment then passed me a number. "Here, this is the lead, Det. Mason Richardson." Then he pointed to his badge number. "Just tell him Tommy Lopushinski says hi."

"Richardson? I'm trying to place him."

"Bill Trevanian's new partner. Jersey guy. Standup guy... a serving member's serving member, like your old man."

"My... you know my father?"

"The Mighty Quinn? Are you kidding me?"

I was beginning to get the impression my father had shielded us from some stuff as kids. We were going to have to talk about that, eventually. "I'll say hello."

"You do that. And give Richardson a call, he'll help you out."

Some cops? They're just good guys. Most, in my experience. They get drug down a lot by the psychos, though. "Thank you, my man," I said. "You didn't have to..."

He waved me off. "Naaah. I used to work in the 35th. Best water ice in the city in that little place just down..."

"Nunzio's," I said. "He puts the extra syrup in. The black currant..."

"You got that right!" he said, pointing with both fingers. "Black currant! Crazy stuff, man."

A moment later his partner crossed the street from an adjacent restaurant with two fresh cups.

"Looks like we're rolling," he said. "Say hello to your brother for me."

After they'd pulled away, I dialed the lead investigator. "Det. Richardson?"

"How can I help you?"

"My name's Liam Quinn. I'm an investigator working on an insurance case I think might be tied to your floaters."

I heard a click, the sound of him starting a recorder. "And where are you right now Mr. Quinn? Can you come in and talk to me about it?"

I chuckled. "Detective, I'm not a secret source. My family are all cops. It's definitely just a related case. No involvement by me."

He cut to the chase. "When can you come in?"

I told him I'd see him in twenty minutes.

Traffic was good, and the Firebird coughed throatily as I punched the engine and headed towards the precinct house. I wasn't looking forward to talking to Bill Trevanian. Like I said before, there was some family history involved.

When I got to the station house, both detectives were standing on the front steps. Richardson was wearing a mismatched corduroy sportscoat and tan trousers but Trevanian was a suit guy, dark blue. They both had their arms crossed, like angry schoolteachers.

I parked the Beast a few feet away in a 'guest' spot. The door had barely swung shut with a fatigued 'thunk' when Trevanian yelled over to me.

"You've got some nerve coming over here to talk to me, you dirty sonuvabitch."

Yeah, like I said: it was going to be a fun little chat.

37.

Two hours later, I was still being interviewed by Richardson and Trevanian.

I told them what I knew, except for the identity of the forger. It wasn't that I distrusted the boys in blue. But they could be less than subtle, and if they picked up Polly Clark before I'd figured this all out, Philadelphia Mutual was out a cool twelve-five, and I was out my healthy fee.

"So, let me get this straight: you think these two guys were capped because they robbed an art gallery for Pat Delaney?"

"Yeah, that's about the size of it."

"But you don't know why they robbed the gallery," Trevanian interjected, "because it might be tied to Delaney's armored car heist, but it might be unrelated."

"Yeah... basically."

"So... after two hours, what you've got is a theory: that somehow Delaney's old partners have come back from the dead and bumped off two schmucks working for him now?"

I nodded.

The older cop leaned back in his chair slightly, looking irritated. "You are some piece of work, you know that?"

"Bill..." Richardson cautioned

"Nahhh... Just let me talk here for a minute," he told his partner. Then he turned his attention back to me. "You get involved in my case, even though you and I have unsettled beef. You go around interviewing suspects for days, without telling me anything. You pass information of some kind to Vincent Terrasini, a fact I know to be true on account of you're still breathing..."

"Detective..."

'DON'T… interrupt me," he said, barely keeping his cool. "You take advantage of a great retired member, Ramon Garcia, to get a license even though you're a conman and a crook, and a dirty little thief."

I shrugged. "I'm six-two. Not so little."

His face went strangely calm, emotionless. He tipped his head slightly and studied me. "Was that a threat, Mr. Quinn?"

"That was a vital statistic, Detective Trevanian. And a relative judgment of size versus the general population, offered in glib tones. My apologies. Don't have a stroke."

That shut him up for a second, if only because he was too angry to talk without doing or saying something he'd regret. Police have to record all interviews these days. There's less leeway to act like they're on the wrong side when the power affords.

Richardson, who by all accounts was a good cop, shot me a foul look indeed. "Mr. Quinn is going to shut up for a minute… please." He addressed Trevanian. "Bill, you want to grab us each a coffee, grab a smoke?"

Trevanian's mouth was hanging open and he was staring down his nose at me like I was roadkill that had just popped a tire. "That might be best," he said.

He rose from his chair without taking his eyes off me, pushed it in then leaned on the back with both hands. "Thank you for choosing to offer your assistance, Mr. Quinn," he said as sincerely as possible. "You can be sure we'll be talking again."

"Was that a thr…" I began to offer back.

"Hey!" Richardson interrupted. "Enough."

Trevanian walked out of the room and it was clear I shouldn't expect any party invites.

"So… Pat Delaney. Pretty thin," Richardson suggested.

I nodded again. "Fortunately," I said, "I'm not the poor bastard who has to figure out what Pat's up to. I just need to find the painting they stole."

He nodded. "And leave the 'charging someone' bit up to us? You ambulance chasers are all heart." It sounded like "haht" in his heavy Philly accent. "Your father would be so proud."

"Hey, I try."

He looked serious for a moment, thinking things over. "There's no way you're telling me everything here, Quinn," he said. "How did you know about the Delaney connection? About his cellmate?"

"Anonymous tip," I said, holding up my cellphone as if it were evidence.

He nodded, but the motion said he didn't believe me. "Right. Well, I'll tell you what: you get any more enlightening phone calls, you make sure you call us first."

38.

After spending most of the day talking to cops, I called
Bryson at the stadium and got contact info for David Mince,
the apparent ringleader in the beer theft.

I figured the easiest way to resolve the whole thing might
be to confront him. He was accustomed to getting his own
way, so I figured losing his sense of control might snap him
around.

That might sound naïve to some; certainly, if you're like
my brother Davy, you'd think so. But I read a lot about
criminology in the prison library, and the truth is there are
two types of sociopath out there, two types of people who
lack empathy for the rest of us, or remorse. Sure, some
people do just seem to be born that way. They show signs at
age two in research. There's all this stuff about how our pre-
frontal cortexes develop differently dramatically changing
how emotional and empathetic people can be.

But most people don't have the issue of sheer biological
impediment. Most criminals are just socially disconnected,
deeply traumatized people who lash out in anger constantly.

They were born with nothing, told or shown that they
were worth nothing and could make nothing, and constantly
surrounded by failure and social dependency. They figure no
one gives a crap about them, so why should they give a crap
back? No one shows them empathy, so they develop none in
return.

If that's not a stacked deck, I don't know what is.

I needed to figure out which kind of mean dude Mince
was: the kind who'd rob you violently then justify it in shrill
tones as the survival of the fittest; or the one who just stabs
someone for the fun of it. If it was column 'b' and he was just

born bad, things were infinitely more complicated.

I told Bryson how I felt about it. "What do you think, chief? You've met the kid more times than me."

He sighed inwardly. "There's something about him sets me off, that's for sure," he said. "He's just a cold, cold fish, man, like he's studying you, dissecting you."

"Looking for weaknesses."

"Yeah. Like... I don't know what, quite. I guess like a hungry animal. Like he might eat you."

"Why didn't you fail his security clearance when they hired him?"

"I couldn't. Can't just fail someone, Mr. Quinn. They need to have a record, or exhibit some kind of threat. Whatever other problems he has, his impulse control seems in check."

That was only fair, I supposed. "Still, you pegged him as cold-blooded."

"Uh-huh," he said. "Cold as they come, that boy."

Mince lived in West Philly in a former subsidized housing block that was one of the few in the neighborhood that hadn't been rescued and turned into a condo block. The wooden front steps were peeling and warped, rocking ever so slightly as I climbed them and the small glass window panel in the dirty and peeling green wood door was shattered.

I didn't need them to buzz me in; the electronic door lock was obviously broken, and the door's spring long gone, so it rested slightly open, like an unused bathroom stall.

Their mailbox said the Mince family was in 4D.

I could hear a racket through the apartment door but two loud knocks got no response. I was about to try again when it flew open, a short, beefy man with greasy light-brown hair standing there in his stained string undershirt and trousers, propping the door fully wide.

"What do you want?" he said, zipping up his pants.

"I'm looking for David."

The guy looked pissed. "You interrupted for that!"

He took a half-step towards me then cocked and threw a right hand in one smooth motion. But I'd seen the anger in his eyes a split-second earlier, and was already feinting backwards, watching his knuckles go flying by, the reaction 'zone' kicking in.

I let his weight carry him slightly past me, so that I could drive my right hand into his right kidney. He groaned and dropped to one knee. As he tried to right himself, I hit him with two crisp jabs, then a right-hand cross.

His head caromed off the door before he hit the floor. His eyelids fluttered, which meant the damage probably wasn't serious, and there were no signs of bleeding.

I stretched my bruised hands and looked past him into the apartment. "Mrs. Mince?"

I walked in cautiously. The light was low, and the lime-green walls shadowed and dirty. The place smelled of acrid smoke and rotting garbage.

In the living room there was just a ratty old brown couch and a television. Mrs. Mince was sitting on the couch in pale blue panties and a rose t-shirt, giggling at a cartoon. She was emaciated; her eyes were rimmed with dark shadows, her lips chapped, her skin pale, the capillaries translucent blue through the tops of her tiny hands.

On the couch next to her she was holding onto a small glass pipe.

"Mrs. Mince, I'm looking for David."

She turned to me like a curious ghoul. "David? David's a good boy. S'got a job; goes to school, and ...." She looked puzzled and blank for a moment, as if trying to recall what she'd been saying ... or even just one more thing about her son of which she could be proud.

I tried to sound reassuring. "I know, Mrs. Mince. I know.

You know where I might find him?"

She shook her head gently. "The Wawa," she said "Hangs out in the back lot..."

"Getting in trouble?"

She waved a hand at me. "Naw. Naw! He's just... he's good. He's a good boy."

"But he gets in lots of fights, right?"

She went to wave the hand again but didn't have the strength to fully follow through in her glassy-eyed state. "Nah. He's good."

I'd have like to have stayed, helped somehow. What do you do in a situation like that? Call... what, social services? She was an adult. She made her own choices, even if not competent, evidently, to do so.

And that was why it was so sad. Because when you really go to know people like Annie Mince, you realized they were broken, typically, long before any of it was their choice. I spent a chunk of time in the stir reading about how the human brain works, how our consciousness and choices are only part of the picture, how our subconscious automatically prompts behavior – without our choosing – when it thinks survival is involved.

And it can get pretty messed up, because the brain adapts, to both good and bad influences.

Mrs. Mince was mentally ill, without a doubt, and an addict, without a doubt. But in America, she was also an adult. Unless she was harming someone else – even something as innocuous as slinging dope herself or attracting dealers to her building – maybe I could've stepped in. But that wasn't how hard-drug dealers worked anymore, for precisely that reason.

She'd bring poison home, her brain telling her it was the closest she would get to medicine, her emotions a muddle of loneliness, separation, social anxiety, depression and self-loathing. Her trauma so deep, her mistrust of people so deep, that there is no fight left. There is no one she wishes to be around, for the sheer risk and the inevitability of being overwhelmed.

The hit of dopamine, the brief, fleeting elevations of her mood to happy, joyous and relaxed? That was the dope, the crack or meth or whatever the Hell had her. That was what she got from it: what the rest of us expect to get from life. To be happy, even for just a few moments. Some strength of will to go on living, for the same brief moments tomorrow. That was all she had – other than her sociopathic, likely brain damaged son, of course.

I headed back down the dingy staircase to the street, to scope out the corner store. It was about four blocks east, and by the time I got close, I could just make out a handful of guys crowded behind it.

They looked like they were out of high school already, big kids. And there were four of them.

I made the mistake of trying to play it cool. General rule, especially in this meme-crazy Internet age: don't do that. Anyone over thirty is like a *Logan's Run* castoff to kids today.

And if that's not a snappy, hip, modern reference, then clearly I don't know what one is.

Clearly.

"Hey fellas!" I said cheerfully.

No reply. One of them was smoking a huge blunt – a joint made with a scooped-out cigar wrapper.

I said, "Anyone here see David Mince?"

A young guy with premature lip hair and a backwards baseball cap went to point down the block, but one of his friends slapped his hands down. "Stupid! Dude is five-oh, man."

I raised both hands, trying to look friendly. "Look, I'm not here to hassle you guys...."

Just then, Mince came around the corner of the building with a six-pack in one hand and a brown paper bag and bottle in the other, the pale red logo belonging to the liquor store down the block. He saw me, but barely acknowledged I was even there, walking over to the other guys and handing them the booze.

"Why're you talking to this guy?"

"Dude is five-oh," one friend said.

Mince squinted derisively. "No, he ain't, he's some security guard or something. He was at the stadium asking questions."

Things weren't looking up.

"What do we do with him?" said the biggest drinking buddy.

Mince shrugged. "I don't care. Stomp him, dip his ass in the river a few times."

Two of them got up. This really wasn't good; I was playing the percentages on Mince letting me walk away able to identify him... and they weren't in my favor. If his friends started stomping, they wouldn't stop until I was dead.

It was time for a little revision of the odds.

Most people will tell you that a five-on-one fight is a done deal, and that the one guy doesn't have a chance. But experience and a sheer brute will to win count a lot in these situations, and you can even up the odds considerably via the element of surprise.

I didn't have time to throw a punch, however. I turned left quickly, placing one flat palm on each side of two of their heads. I slammed them together and put both down, hard.

"Mother..." the largest guy, still standing, began to say. I threw a hard right elbow backwards, catching him in the throat. He fell to the ground gasping for air, and before Mince could even take a step, the odds were down to two-on-one.

The two of them took a hesitant step. As I waved a finger to ward them both off, I gave one of the groaning, prone youths an unhealthy, short kick.

"Now, you two might be able to take me, still," I told the pair. "But I doubt it." I nodded towards Mince's friend. "By the time you get that piece out of your pocket, you'll be out, too."

He looked down at his friends, then he looked at Mince.... and then he ran, as fast as his pricey high-tops could take him. His sneakers clopped across the street as he turned the corner and disappeared from sight.

Mince seemed unfazed even by losing his supporting crew. "You think you're pretty badass, don't you?" he said. "Go ahead: hit me."

I already knew Mince was a minor. The other guys were self-defence. Otherwise, I'd have taken him up on it.

Instead, I said, "No thanks, kid. I think maybe life has knocked you around enough already."

He dropped his fists. "What do you want?"

"I want you to return the beer you helped steal, and I want you to leave DeShawn and Jeffrey alone."

"Or what? You're going to beat up some more of my friends?"

He was a smug little sociopath, but he'd given me an idea.

I turned to leave.

"Hey. Hey! Where the hell are you going?" he said.

I turned and smiled over my shoulder. "I know someone who'll have far more effect talking to you about this stuff than I could. I'm going to give him a call," I said.

He crossed his arms defiantly as his friends crawled to mobility again and licked their wounds.

"Yeah? Get bent," he said, as I walked away.

"I'll see you real soon, David," I said.

39.

I ALREADY HAD A THEORY on what the young Brit forger Polly Clark was up to. But I wouldn't get a chance to confirm it until she made a move. Fortunately, Danny was doing a half-decent job for a change, and had her under wraps constantly.

She was quiet as mouse, which is why it struck him as odd when, after taking a long phone call, she lit out of her store like her shoes were on fire and the parking lot was water.

"That was as close to sprinting as she's ever going to get," he said hurriedly over the phone, a few seconds after she took off.

"Follow her, Danny. I'll pick up the tab for your gas and food, just don't lose her. I'm going to head over to her store while she's out."

The drive took nearly twenty-five minutes because of traffic, and by the time I walked around the back of her store in the dilapidated strip mall to see if I could get in without breaking and entering, Danny had followed her back into town, to the 30th Street Amtrak train station.

He was breathless, walking as he talked. "I don't know Quinn, she doesn't seem like the Amtrak type to me."

Danny would know; he'd been running petty scams at the train station for years, now and again.

"She's not there to catch a train. Call the cops, now. Ask for Det. Richardson. Get him down there, and tell him I said his floaters will make sense if he meets you there – and bring backup."

"Huh? His whatsy-what now?"

"His floaters will make sense. Look, just tell him. I'll be there as soon as I can."

I hung up then walked over to the back door. From his description, she'd bolted from the store without locking up – not that she had much worth stealing. I figured it came about five seconds after she'd heard about the failed swimming lesson featuring Delaney's old cellmate.

Sure enough, the back door was unlocked. She hadn't even flipped over the open sign of the front door, so they'd have a hard time even making trespassing stick.

In the long run, it wouldn't matter. If I was right, the cops would be all over the place soon anyway.

On one of her two large art tables I found what I was looking for: the Dufresne copy, pulled from its mounting and frame, crumpled up in a ball. I left it where I was, careful not to touch anything in the store before heading back to my car.

It was time to be grateful for driving the Firebird; I probably gave half the other drivers on the road heart attacks making time back to Philly.

I didn't doubt Polly had already found what she was looking for by the time I got to the station, and I bolted past the main doors and the giant columns that preceded the huge, marble-floored main waiting area.

I headed towards the lockers, keeping an eye out for Danny. When I spotted him, he was around the corner on a short corridor to the bathrooms, keeping an eye on Polly as she fumbled with a key to a locker door. I'd wondered where they'd stashed that stolen armored car loot. I'd figured on a locker somewhere, as they can be rented long-term and retrieved by more than one person.

He had to stash the loot somewhere. That had been taken care of when he'd initially considered fleeing by Amtrak, only to find too many police about the station. Instead, he'd used the lockers there for the duffel bag full of cash.

The key to that locker was another matter. The painting made sense once I realized that was half of it... and that Pat Delaney, on the run, had access to it.

She'd retrieved the key from the frame in which he'd stashed it... unwittingly, also the frame his old lady used for the Dufresne copy. She'd made the copy for Vin the Shin, so his man could steal the original, and in doing so, given away her boyfriend's meal ticket.

The original Dufresne, stolen from Vin the Shin, had replaced the copy on the gallery wall. Pat and his buddies got their payday and the Vermeer.

Maybe.

That latter part bothered me, still. The key made sense for them, as it led to cold, hard cash. But Pat was no art expert or fence.

Danny saw me walk into the station and flicked his head in the direction of the opposite wall.

Across the huge hall, past the drifting commuters, Teddy and two pals were watching Polly, too.

Things were going to get ugly quickly if the cops didn't get there soon.

They noticed us at about the same time, Teddy jerking his head in my direction, then whispering to one of his men. I doubted they'd be unarmed this time; and Teddy had a shrewd look on his face, like maybe he'd figured a guy like me wouldn't carry a piece.

Sure enough, a few seconds later they both jogged towards her, Teddy's nine-millimeter Smith & Wesson coming out of his pocket. She'd just about managed to extract the huge duffle bag from the locker when he jammed it into the small of her back, spinning her around just in time for me to get there.

"You got a good right hand, kid, but I got the range this

time," he said. "I'd think real hard about testing the odds here."

I nodded towards them. "Only way you'd ever get a shot off at me," I said.

"You caught me a little flatfooted, that's all. I'll know better if we ever go again."

"Teddy, you could have six sets of toes, and you'd still be too slow for me."

He smiled when I used his name. "I'm guessin' if you know who I am you already figured this all out, right?"

"Pretty much, yeah."

"So you know there's no freakin' way I'm leaving here without this knapsack, right?"

"I hear you've got about two-point-three million reasons to hang onto it," I said. "That was the take in that armored car heist, right?"

His eyes flitted about, scanning the room for a moment. "Okay, here's what we're going to do: my friends and I are going to take little miss artistic here along as some insurance. I hear you're a real sweetheart, so I'm guessing you don't want us to shoot her in the kidneys, right?"

"One thing I don't get," I asked. "How come you guys didn't try to get the money before now?"

He snickered. "You wouldn't believe me."

I needed to kill time, wait out the cavalry. "So try me."

"Would you believe, honor among thieves? We was just waiting out Pat, waiting for him to get paroled. Then he up and pulled a fast one; his cellmate got out and Pat put him up to ripping us off."

"And you introduced him to the refreshing depths of the Delaware River, inconveniently attached to an anchor."

He shrugged. There were plenty of other passengers milling around the station, but no one within earshot. "It's nothing personal," said Teddy. "It's just business. Pat would even agree, if he weren't stuck inside for another three-to-five."

"When you guys all go down for this, he's going to get another dime at least. You'll get life for those two goombahs. Hope it was worth it."

That annoyed him. "You talk too much. You know what? I'm thinking maybe you should come along for a little ride, too." He pointed the gun at my head then shook it in the direction of the door. "Time to go, Quinn," he said.

He led us out, the gun on Polly's back and his two friends behind us. They hadn't spotted Danny yet, and I saw him out of the corner of my eye, moving along the side of the room cautiously, towards the exit.

"When we get outside, there's a white Chevy parked in the loading zone. Quinn, you're getting in the back ahead of me."

I didn't know how he was going to do it, but Danny needed to give us a distraction, a chance for me to take one or two of them down and even things up a little, get that gun off of Polly's back.

We walked towards the car, the cops nowhere in sight yet, although for a faint second the sound of approaching sirens made everyone look around. "Must be close," said Teddy. "Get in."

Danny's timing was perfect. Just as the other thug pulled down on the handle, a pair of red dice rolled directly in front of Teddy, sliding and tumbling gracefully across the cement – Snake Eyes, which was good enough for me. As both men looked down at the dice, I flung the door open quickly, knocking down the one guy, then stamped on Teddy's toes as hard as I could, praying they weren't steel-toed shoes.

The cracking noise said they weren't. He howled in pain and jumped a half-foot backwards on his one good foot, trying to train the nine millimeter on me at the same time, with predictable consequences, his balance going out from under him and a shot flying randomly into the air. He went over backwards, his head cracking loudly off the asphalt.

The third gunman was going for his pocket.

I kicked down hard on his kneecap, blowing it instantly out of place. He yowled in pain, clutching at it.

The goon by the car had recovered his balance and didn't even go for his gun, as the sirens wailed closer. Instead, he pulled out a switchblade. "Come on! Come on!" he said, waving it in a wild arc.

In the movies, the good guy kicks the knife out of the bad guy's hands. Unless you're a ballet dancer or pro soccer player, this is easier said than done, and I backed away twice as he took two more quick swings. "Not so smart now, are you…" he said.

"Smart enough to know that siren's just around the corner, tough guy," I said, gesturing with my head towards the next cross street.

And just like that, he made things easy on me by looking back at the source of the wail. The punch was coming in on him before he could even fully turn back to face me. My first jab broke his nose, filling his eyes with tears so that he couldn't see. The second was a body shot, doubling him over.

And, I got to practice my uppercut one more time. Like I said back when all this started, looking down at Abel Larsson on that pool room floor, it's never been my best punch. But Teddy's pal was leaning forward when I cut loose, and I'd swear his cheap black dress shoes actually came an inch off the ground.

I'd lost sight of Polly. She'd grabbed the knapsack and was sprinting down the street, but hadn't gotten more than fifty yards when the cruisers peeled around the corner, klaxons and lights blaring.

She stuttered to a stop, then tried the other direction and

saw us, stuttering to a stop again … until the heel of her right shoe came right off. "Buger!" she said. "Bugger, bugger, bugger!" She kicked off her shoes. Running between traffic was out of the question; she turned towards the station... just in time to be greeted by the rest of the boys in blue.

Polly froze in place, her arms dropping to her side, handbag suspended lamely.

40.

An hour later, we were still at the scene, each of us getting a quick questioning independently of one another in the back of a cruiser, so police could get the freshest versions possible, see where the stories gelled and where they didn't.

The onlooking witnesses got to talk to the handful of uniformed officers. Det. Richardson took care of mine personally.

"Now, I have to think when we talked the other day, Mr. Quinn, you were holding out on me a little bit."

I shook my head. "Detective. Partner not here for the happy moment?"

"Answer the question."

"Why would I hold anything back? Where would you get an idea like that? Geez."

Just then, a reporter leaned through the car window, to shoot video of us talking.

"Hey! Respect the police cordon, please," the cop said.

The video shooter backed away.

I gestured towards the media. "Doesn't look like I did you too much harm. You guys are going to come out of this looking like geniuses."

"I don't get it," he said. "How did you know what she was up to?"

"You kind of had to be there," I said. It was a hell of a long story. "How long have you got?"

It took me the better part of twenty minutes to explain everything to the incredulous Richardson, who took off his old-school fedora and pinched the bridge of his nose.

"Who would have figured? Pat Delaney masterminding another heist from inside."

"His unfortunate cellmate just wasn't clear on the threat

level Pat's former associates posed, I guess," I said. "You might find those nines they're packing match up with whatever they used to clip your floaters."

Richardson rolled down his side window again and lit a smoke. "You don't mind? I've had four this week, you know."

"Cigarettes?"

"Hell, no. I wish. Floaters."

"Rough."

He took a deep drag then blew a perfect ring out the window. "I should really quit these horrible things. My wife smells the tobacco on me, she goes out of her mind."

I let him talk. Cases like this? There was no end of talking after them. Better to get accustomed to it.

"You know, I looked you up. You've done pretty good since getting out. In fact, you got a better closure rate than a lot of flatfoots I know."

I had to smile at that. Then it occurred to me he probably knew my old man.

"Yeah, The Mighty Quinn," he laughed. "Ask him about that one." Then his expression shifted to befuddlement. "Wait a second... you said this all started with the gallery robbery on Chestnut?"

"Yeah..."

"But what about the other picture? You said there was two that went missing. You've told me what happened to the first one, the fake. What about the Vermeer, the real deal...?"

I nodded. "Yeah, that bit's interesting. I'm not entirely sure yet."

He rolled his eyes and I got the sense he didn't believe me. "Now, you've lied to me on this once already, Quinn. Don't let the fact that your old man and me go back fool you into thinking I won't run your ass in if you blow this for us."

"Just do me a favor," I said.

"Depending."

"Anyone asks you how you guys knew this was going down, it was an anonymous tip, okay? None of the actual story. That way, if anyone gets loose lipped..."

Richardson had been around a while. "Gotcha. But... Quinn, goddamn it, why would you be asking me to keep things quiet if you didn't know anything about the other painting?"

"Detective, have I done anything so far but make you look good?"

He frowned. But, like I said, Richardson had been around for a while. "Fine, but you don't wrap this up quick, I'm coming after an explanation. Or I'm sending Trevanian. You don't want that."

"You do that 'intimidation' thing really well. You could play the gruff police captain in an eighties action comedy."

Richardson momentarily closed his eyes and took in a lungful of air. "When you were a kid, your old man used to come to the tavern and tell us what a pain in the ass you were. If his liver ever fails, I wouldn't necessarily blame the state of crime in Philly for it."

"You know I'm seeing him in a couple of hours. You want I should say hello?"

"Better yet," he said, "where are you drinking?"

"Druid."

He nodded and smiled. "What my old lady don't know, you know? I swear, working homicide is the best job ever, because at least 50% of the jerks you deal with are dead."

I finished up with Richardson and got out of his cruiser, then hoofed it a block to the Beast. My phone rang just as I was pulling away from the train station.

"Given that there are police cars all over the neighborhood around 30th Street station, and given that I am to understand you were there, am I to also understand you have something to tell me, Quinn?" Vin the Shin asked.

Ah, hell. I had to call him soon enough anyway. "Yeah. Good news, I tracked down the two guys who knocked over your condo."

"This is good news indeed, young bull. I feel my temper subsiding at a rate of which my doctor would approve."

"Bad news, they're both already dead."

The line was silent for a moment. "That's ... unfortunate."

"Yeah, but if it's any consolation, the two guys that clipped them are sitting about a hundred yards away from me right now in the back of a cruiser."

He was quiet again for a moment, but then said, "Quinn, I thought I made it clear that I was to hear about these two before anyone else."

"They were already dead by the time I heard about them," I said. "Cops fished them out of the river yesterday."

That seemed to satisfy him a little. "As I said, unfortunate. Still, I owe you one for keeping an eye out for me," the gang boss said. "You should come by my club. I'll set you up with one of the girls, a private room."

His timing couldn't have been better – but I wasn't going anywhere near his skanky champagne room. "Actually, sir, I can use a smaller favor."

Vin the Shin sounded surprised. "You don't say?"

41.

A half-hour later, Vincent Terrasini's black Lincoln stretch limousine was pulling up outside of David Mince's building.

I knew the teen sociopath wasn't going to listen to me and I sat on the front seat, next to his driver, separated by the raised chauffeur's divider. But Terrasini had left the audio on between the two compartments.

"You comfy up there, Quinn?"

"Yes sir, Mr. Terrasini," I said.

"Good. I'll have a word with the kid, and everybody's happy. Now let's get this over with. Paulie, go get the kid. If he's not there, find out where he is. Quinn, does he got a car?"

"No, Mr. Terrasini, I don't think so."

"Good," he said, crossing his fingers contentedly on his stomach. He could have been someone's grandfather, out for an afternoon drive. But if anyone could scare David Mince straight, it was Vin the Shin.

A few minutes later, the door opened, and Paulie shoved Mince into the car. I listened over the intercom, trying to peek through the smoked glass – raised at the mob boss's insistence, and without an argument from me.

For the first few seconds, no one said anything. Then Terrasini spoke up.

"You know who I am?"

Silence. I assumed Mince was nodding. Very few people in Philadelphia could have avoided knowing Vin the Shin.

"Good. Then you know that I'm a serious man, David, and I insist upon being taken as such. Now... open your mouth."

"What…." Mince exclaimed.

There was the sound of struggling, as Paulie held the kid in place. Then the mobster spoke again, his voice low, menacing.

"You feel that barrel against the back of your mouth, David? You go turn yourself in for the beer job, or the next time, Paulie pulls the trigger and blows your brains out. And after the cops and the courts deal with you, you make nice until you're out of school, or the next time, Paulie pulls the trigger, and blows your brains out. Got it? Nod slowly if you do, 'Cause we don't want him to do it accidentally…. Good."

There was silence for a moment again, then the sound of Terrasini lighting a cigarette, the familiar click of a Zippo lighter opening, a moment later snapping shut. Terrasini said, "You know, it's funny. Because most kids your age, they'd be a hell of a lot more scared right now. I got a feeling you don't feel too much of anything, do you, kid?"

Again, Mince said nothing, but I could have sworn the gangster's voice was tinged with admiration. "That's it, isn't kid? I know a little about this, 'Cause I'm in a tough business, where it don't pay to feel too much. So maybe you do what I tell you now, and in a year, maybe you come back and talk to me about what you're going to do with the rest of your life."

"Okay," the boy said simply.

"There's a good kid. Now get out of my car."

I heard the limo door open and closed, and watched through the passenger side as David went back into his building. The partition whirred and lowered.

"So there you go, Quinn, you get your favor."

I wasn't sure what to say. I hadn't really counted on him offering the kid a job. He read my reaction and said, "Hey, I see promise in the kid. He's a stone-cold killer that one." Then he gave me another hard stare. "You look shocked, Quinn."

I said, "I'm sorry Mr. Terrasini, I just…"

He waved a hand. "Fuhgeddaboudit. Think about it this way: would you rather have the David Minces of the world taking care of our dirty business, or capping John and Jane Q. Public?"

Before I could answer, he added, "And you don't get 'neither' as an option in the real world. Speaking of which … what about you, kid? You need some steady work?"

I politely declined. "Insurance business is good to me, Mr. Terrasini. I'm going to stick with that for a while."

He puffed on his cigarette, looking happy with himself. "I know how that feels. Insurance business has been pretty good to me, too."

And that made Paulie and his chunky colleague both jiggle with laughter.

Terrasini said, "You change your mind, you give me a call, kid. If this Mince kid works out for me, I still owe you."

I nodded. Then it occurred to me. "We can clear that up really quickly, sir. Do you have business with a guy named Carl Hecht? He's got some stake in the gallery that was robbed, and I'm interested to know what; a friend of mine's job might depend on it."

If things worked out the way I hoped with Vin the Shin, John DeGoey would finally be off the hook with the Hecht brothers… and I could get back to the question of who walked away with a Johannes Vermeer original.

QUINN CHECKS IN

42.

Carl Hecht's approach in muscling out John DeGoey was so old-school mob – offer a helping hand then leverage that debt like a sponge with a vice-grip on water – that it just made sense for there to be a connection, and to use my one favor to ask about him.

Of course, that kind of operation isn't too different from what happens on Wall Street daily, although crossing a 'made' guy in Philly tended to result in more immediate damage.

Vin the Shin said he'd never liked his nephew, didn't think he was sincere. He had no problem loosening the screws on John DeGoey. "He's a little weasel," was his way of putting it over the phone. "Yeah, I'll tell him to end that little venture right quick. Piss him right off."

I'd asked him what that would mean for Hecht, and Terrasini sounded unimpressed. "What do you mean what does it mean for him? How would I know?" he'd said. "I wouldn't bet on him walking away from the whole thing with too much money, though. Knowing Johnny, he'd be lucky just to walk away."

I'd figured that would get Johnny Terrasini and Carl Hecht off DeGoey's back and save Alison's job. Anyone warned off by Vin the Shin would be smart enough to just walk away and lick his wounds.

Evidently not. Hecht had called me a couple of hours later. I'd just finished showering and changing after working out at the gym and was walking back to the Beast when my phone rang.

"What's the deal?"

"What deal?"

"Maybe you tell me."

215

"Again, you're on the vague end of the spectrum ...."

"Friend of mine says you got some powerful friends of your own. I want to know why you're involved in my business. Five o'clock, at the Golden Dragon on East Wadsworth."

Then he hung up.

East Wadsworth is not exactly what you'd call upscale, mostly brick low-rises rented out to small businesses barely making it. So, I wasn't entirely comfortable with the arrangements. But like I said: who figures a crooked business guy like Hecht for taking on a friend of Vin the Shin? No one, that's who. And he thought I was a friend of Terrasini's, no doubt.

The Golden Dragon was an old neighborhood fried rice joint. I'd never noticed it before, just a million others like it, a small storefront with fading gold lettering on peeling red paint.

I was three feet from the front door when the window exploded under the hail of bullets. The black SUV had pulled up on the other side of the road, a handful of men opening fire, the shattered fragments of glass cascading over the sidewalk. Of course, unlike in the movies, in real life the average handgun just isn't that accurate from thirty feet away, and so all the drive-by managed to do was raise the cost of the restaurant owner's glass coverage.

Realizing they'd pull up with traffic behind them, I took off in the other direction. Unable to U-turn into the oncoming lane, two of them had bailed out after me.

As the sidewalk flew by, the soles of my shoes clacked loudly, only partly drowned out by the heaviness of my breath. I was in good shape, but the pair chasing me evidently were, too, and they had guns... and we'd been running for close to ten straight minutes.

North Philly has lots of little ethnic enclaves, and in this one just off Michener Avenue, the folks were mostly from the Caribbean and Africa. On a better day, when the rain wasn't cutting lightly across a bleak late afternoon sky, I might've been up here with Nora, getting some fine jerk chicken and curry. Despite some of the more paranoid and bitter city residents referring to neighborhoods near here as "North Killadelphia," experience has taught me there are good and bad everywhere.

For now, I had to keep sharp, rounding a corner off East Vernon and sprinting down Forrest Street past what looked like an old red brick church. The mesh fences were rusted here and the neighborhood had been getting progressively worse throughout the chase, but the properties and terrain felt wide open compared to the small lots downtown, and I couldn't figure how I was going to lose them.

I cut behind some row houses, where a group of kids were gathered smoking weed. They instinctively looked to bolt, but I called out. "Yo! Who wants to make fifty bucks? I've got two cops chasing me."

The leader of the group, a tall kid with a serious look and a black Nike sweatshirt, stepped up. "You got the fifty?"

I pulled out my wallet and peeled off three twenties. "How about we make it sixty?"

The kids smiled.

It couldn't have been more than twenty seconds later when the pair rounded the corner after me, two muscular, fit middle-aged white guys in non-descript single-breasted suits., both with their pieces drawn. They were exactly what the kids expected … even if they weren't actually cops.

There must have been about a dozen kids, and as I crouched behind two trash cans, they gathered in front of them, hiding me efficiently.

The older one had a moustache. "You kids see a guy run by here a minute ago, tall, athletic?"

"He look like you?"

"No, younger."

"I meant he a white dude?"

The other kids laughed. I peeked through the group as the older thug shoulder-holstered his gun.

Obviously, Hecht had set me up for a hit, and it occurred to me that maybe Johnny Terrasini wasn't so worried about his uncle anymore.

I figured if I tapped either of these guys and drug them down to the cop shop, they wouldn't say jack, not unless they wanted the same treatment from a handful of other guys.

My problem now was two-fold, as the confused pair backed away from the group and started scanning up and down the road again: first, I'd parked across the street from the restaurant, making running back to my car impossible when the gunfire went down. So, I had to get back there without the rest of the crew in the SUV spotting me.

Second, I had to shake the two guys standing ten feet away.

As you might have figured by now, fights in real life tend to be short and brutal. It's a matter of necessity: someone nearly always has a weapon on them, and if one side doesn't knock the other senseless quickly, someone's probably going to get killed by that weapon.

As I don't carry a gun – and am not allowed to by the state, it should be noted – this generally puts me at a disadvantage. Sticking to that core concept of finishing things quickly is especially important.

The two were facing opposite ways down the street, about twenty feet away. I motioned for the kids to keep quiet then grabbed their basketball, walking calmly towards the two. Before they could turn, I nailed the guy to my right with a hard chest pass into the back of his head, momentarily stunning him.

The noise prompted his partner to swing quickly towards me. But I'd already run four or five paces towards him, so he was really just turning into the punch.

As hard as he went down, we weren't done – his buddy had gotten up from his knees and was scrambling to grab his snub-nose .38, which landed about six feet away. I took a running kick at his chin as he reached for it, hitting it square enough to hammer him backwards, hitting the concrete sidewalk with a satisfying thud.

A few feet away, the kids' basketball was slowly rolling. I grabbed it and tossed it back to them. "Thanks."

The biggest kid nodded towards the two unconscious goons. "They really five-oh?" he said.

I shrugged. "I wouldn't recommend waiting around until they wake up to find out," I said before heading back to East Wadsworth at a sprint.

By the time I reached my car, I'd spotted the SUV rounding the neighborhood twice. Unfortunately, before I could unlock the beast's door and jump in, they'd spotted me. They pulled up to the sidewalk and two more men jumped out. With a handful of pedestrians around, neither had his piece out, but they ran towards me from just under a block away.

Fleeing was getting monotonous. I bolted a half block and peeked over my shoulder. Both were older, but trying hard to keep up. I turned down a side street and a sign caught my eye across the road. "The Island Sun." Where had I heard that before?

Dufresne, the artist. His parents' place.

I sprinted across the street and into the attached bookstore, peeking back out the front door window just in time to see them round the corner after me and come to a screeching halt, trying to figure out my new direction.

From behind me, a warm woman's voice said. "Can I

help you?"

I looked sheepish. "Uh, yeah. Sorry."

"You in some sort of trouble?"

I waggled my head back and forward, weighing my answer. "Yeah, I guess you could say that. You don't know Clinton Dufresne by any chance?"

"I gave birt' to him, so I'm betting I do," she said sternly.

"Uh. Yeah. Sorry. I'm an investigator, working on that gallery theft…"

"He told us. It scared hell out of us. But why are ya starin' out the windah?"

"Bad guys."

"'Ow bad?"

"Shoot me dead bad."

She chewed her lip for a moment. "I grow up in Kingston," she said. "I know all sort of good people get caught up. Ya come back 'ere to the office be'ind the register."

I tilted my head and examined her with a smile. "Clinton has a nice mother."

"And that's why he a nice boy," she said seriously.

She was right about that, too.

By the time I'd managed to get out of north Philly, Hecht had called me back.

He didn't even wait for me to ask who it was. "Look, nothing personal," he said. "It wasn't my call."

"Really?"

"Yeah, well… you pissed off that partner of mine that you called in a favor on. You know, from Vin the Shin."

"Not really a favor…"

"Could have fooled me. Him too, I imagine."

"I just wanted you to leave this one guy alone. Is that so tough?"

"Not for me. For my partner? He's not big on ultimatums. He is one upset guy. I'm even contemplating getting out of town myself."

Straight to the point. "And how serious would you say his level of annoyance is with me, Mr. Hecht?"

"I'd say if you were still inside the joint, you wouldn't make it through lunch without a shiv in the back."

"Don't sound so happy about it."

"Oh, don't get me wrong: I don't give a damn if he whacks you. I just don't think it's good for business. So, you got Mr. DeGoey a little help. It's all good. Life goes on, you know? Well ... my life goes on, anyway."

And then he hung up.

Funny guy.

But not that funny. Johnny Terrasini, openly defying his uncle? That didn't sound good at all. In this town, that kind of rival stuff usually meant bullets flying two ways. And even though I wasn't involved... I was now involved.

But the incident got me thinking about Alison Pace, and her having to deal with rich sociopaths.

And that got me thinking about that missing Vermeer. Instead of putting my phone away, I dialled a number back.

"Deputy Warden McArthur."

"Sir, it's Liam Quinn calling back. I was wondering; that list I looked at before, of Pat Delaney's visitors...?"

"Sure, what about it?"

"That permission didn't expire or anything? I need to check one more thing."

43.

I headed back downtown, calling Nora and Alison along the way, and getting both to invite everyone down to the Druid. It was time to fill them in on everything that had gone down. They'd doubtless already heard about Teddy Armas and Polly Clark being booked but would have no way of knowing about Patrick Delaney's connection, what with him still being in jail.

And there was still the matter of the missing Vermeer.

But first I went home. I'd bruised the hell out of my knuckles for the second time in three days, and they needed ice. Plus, I had to check if my neighbor Ricky was okay, and fill Vin the Shin in on his treacherous little nephew.

I parked the Firebird in the underground lot and took the elevator up to my floor. As the door was opening, Ricky was just locking his door to go out, maybe to see Al downstairs.

"Ricky, hey. Look, I just wanted…'

He held up a hand. "Talk to it, Liam." Then he walked by me and hit the elevator button for a down car.

"Ricky…"

He gave me a quick, hurt look. "I've been beat up enough times in my life already by ignorant bigots, Liam," he said. "I don't need that crap where I live, you know? And you don't even come by and talk to me about it for two days?"

He was right. You might feel awkward, or guilty, or lousy. But when you've done a friend wrong, you don't walk by his door without stopping to talk, and that's exactly what I'd done.

"I got caught up in the case," I said. "I'm sorry man, really…"

He held up the hand again. "Just... stop. I don't want to hear it, okay? You really hurt my feelings man and I just don't want to even talk to you right now, you know?"

And then he marched into the elevator. I motioned to come after him and he shook his head seriously then pushed the button to close the doors.

Damn.

In my apartment, my phone messages had stacked up. My mother tended to only use land lines still – modern technology wasn't really her thing – and she'd left about twenty to make sure I wasn't going to miss Sunday dinner two weeks in a row.

Alison Pace had left one, too.

"Hey... Look, I'm sorry if I came on a bit strong the other night. I just thought you should know I'm going to try and work things out with Leo. I know he can be a bit of a dog, but we've been together two years, you know? Anyway, I got Nora's message, so I guess I'll see you tonight at the Druid? Okay. Well ... bye Liam."

Even after the chase and the fight – such as it was – I still had nervous tension to wear off. I put on the TV and listened to a repeat of Conan from the night before, as I ran through some stretches and a light workout. Then, while Andy ran Conan's tie through an electric cheese grater, I turned the volume down and called Vin the Shin.

His nephew's betrayal didn't seem to faze him.

"So... you want a medal for telling me this? You think I owe you a favor? I already did you a favor."

Wise guys can be exasperating to deal with. "Look, I just thought you should know: he set me up, and was making noises about coming after you. At least that's what Hecht said."

He was silent for a few moments then took a deep breath. "You know, I've been real nice to everybody what pissed me off this week," he said, his voice raised to near a yell. "Pretty soon, that's going to end!"

I didn't say anything. Even on the phone line, it would've been like poking a bear with a real long reach.

He sighed again. "Sorry kid. I don't mean nothing by it, you know? You done good telling me about this. Just keep your head down, okay? I can't look after you, even with Johnny gunning for me. He's a 'made' guy, which means it's hands off for me when it comes to keeping him away from you, you understand?"

I understood. Vin the Shin was telling me I didn't have a leg to stand on.

"One thing I would suggest, kid, is getting out of that apartment. It didn't take us too damn long to find it. Dumb as my nephew is, I'm sure one of his guys can use Google, and one of the other ones can read it to him."

After we got off the phone, I watched the rest of Conan and put my swollen right hand in some ice. The knuckles were raw and one had split the skin, leaving a smear of blood that ran up my middle finger, like an angry salute.

44.

Two hours later I got to the Druid. It was only eight o'clock, but the joint was humming already. Even the regular bar stools were crowded out. I saw my father by the near wall, with his cronies, and after he gave me a congratulatory backslap, I whispered in his ear for a second and caught him up to speed.

I spotted Nora across the room, in the far corner, with a small group using the broke-down old player piano as a rest area. "Liam!" she exclaimed, coming over to hug me. "I heard you did good!"

Marty the bartender was busy wiping down the bar. I told him to expect a little help. "You mentioned you needed a hand."

"Yeah?"

"I've got a kid coming over tomorrow. His name's DeShawn. Nice boy but not the brightest candle on the cake, you know?"

"DeShawn? Don't sound very Irish," said Marty.

I cocked an eyebrow at him. "Your last name is DiSilvio. What are you worrying about?"

He thought about it. "I guess you got me there. Kid can work every weekend?"

"Every single one. Hard-working kid, Marty. Just needs a break. Easily led on by the bad kids."

He thought about it some more. "Sure. Okay, I'll give him a shot."

About ten feet away, Alison and Leo were talking to my brother Andy, who'd made a rare appearance, collar and all. I motioned for the two of us to go over and join them, and when Fiona the waitress went by, I bothered her for a pint of Smithwicks.

"Andy," I said, giving him a brotherly nod. "Isn't tomorrow your work day?"

"Oh, very funny you are; a regular Shameless O. Tool."

Alison laughed daintily, bell-like, and tossed her chestnut-auburn hair. "What does the 'O' stand for?"

Andy downed the last of his beer then used the empty glass as a pointer. "In Liam's case it's "Oh my God, what a useless twat I am."

I nodded towards him. "You can see why he's a man of the cloth, with that mouth."

Andy, without missing a beat, liberated a new half-pint from Fiona's. "Well," he said, "I should damn well hope so."

My father quietened everyone. "All right, all right, you heathens," he said. "I just wanted to announce that thanks to my boy Liam, that bastard Pat Delaney won't be getting out again for a very long time. So I want us to raise a glass."

He did, and the rest of the room followed suit.

"Speech!" someone yelled from the back.

"Yeah, come on jailbird," someone else called out, to laughs.

I pretended to wave them away, but they persisted, which set the stage pretty well.

"Okay, settle down," I said. "Settle down. Geez, what a bunch of useless drunks you are!"

The room erupted in laughs again, glasses clinking, more than a few being tipped and drained.

"I just want to say I couldn't have figured out Pat's connection without help from everyone who was at the DeGoey Fine Arts Gallery when it was robbed, and I particularly want to thank Alison Pace, the gallery's manager," I said.

She got a polite round of applause and raised an

embarrassed half-wave in my direction.

I continued. "As for the missing painting, the Vermeer, that was a different matter," I said.

She looked puzzled. "What do you mean?"

"Well, indirectly, that one was on you," I said.

A murmur went around the room, and Alison looked genuinely puzzled.

"Liam, I don't know what you think you've figured out, but I didn't steal that painting. And I didn't hire anyone else to, either."

I smiled. "I know. But your boyfriend Leo did."

Again, a gasp went around the room. Alison took a reflexive half-step away from him.

Leo looked around for a moment, confused. Then he faced me. "I don't know what the hell he's talking about."

Following our short earlier discussion, my father had three of his friends blocking the exits. But Leo didn't bolt. He must have figured that without the painting having been recovered, he couldn't get caught, with an accomplice who was already in jail.

"When we first talked," I said, "you mentioned you were involved in three cases in the last nine months that were so big they put Walter Beck on the front page."

"Yeah? So?"

"So, one of those three cases was the armored car heist pulled off by Pat Delaney and his partners."

He snorted. "Coincidence. You got nothing."

"Coincidence? So it's also a coincidence that Delaney's cellmate was knocked off yesterday by the guys he worked with on the armored car heist, and that they were then recovered with the money? That's coincidence?"

"It would seem so."

"The first time we talked, you said you didn't know anything about art other than what Alison told you. And yet you were also cheating with the girlfriend of the guy who owned the Vermeer, Paul Dibartolo, who I saw coming out of your place. Another coincidence?"

Now he was getting nervous, so I continued. "When Pat Delaney's men robbed that place, they wanted one thing: the train station locker key he had unwittingly hidden in Polly Clark's frame of a forged painting, not knowing she was about to give that painting to ... an interested third party, to complete a theft of his own.

"It was literally the key to millions of dollars for them. But instead of getting in and out as quickly as possible, Delaney's men stopped in the gallery and grabbed one other painting – the one painting your girlfriend, the gallery manager had told you about, that you knew was valuable. Your own words."

Leo wasn't sure what to do. "You can't prove any of this. You've got nothing, Quinn," he said.

"Yeah? Well, I wondered about that. I wondered how it was that Pat Delaney could have found out about the gallery having the Dufresne and set up the robbery without help from someone on the outside. And you were sleeping with Paul Dibartolo's girlfriend as well, so you knew what the Vermeer was worth. I also know Polly Clark doesn't visit anymore, but she was in this up to her eyeballs, which meant there had to be a go-between. So my dad called a friend of his at State Corrections and had a check on Pat Delaney's visitor list over the last month. Who do you think the only visitor's name to come up was?"

"Not mine." He smiled glibly.

"No, not yours. That got me, too. I had to think on that one for a while. Then I remembered that certificate on your apartment wall. 'Leonard Piddle', if I recall correctly. And – let's be really frank here, that's not a name you easily forget. Leo Tesser didn't visit Pat Delaney in the slam. But Leonard

Piddle sure did."

Now he knew he was done. But he could also see three old, retired cops blocking the doors, and Leo surprised me: he pulled a pistol from his waistband, raising it with both hands. In the absent-minded fearful disconnection of the moment, I realized it was a Glock, like my brother Davy's service piece.

Geez. Everyone and anyone is packing these days.

"Everybody get down!" he screamed, swinging it towards both sides of the room.

You never saw thirty-five people duck so quickly.

But Nora was still standing next to him. In his panicked rage, Leo had forgotten the women on either side of him. "Oh, the hell you don't!" she said, nailing him with a hard right. Leo's eyes rolled back, and he stumbled a bit, glassily.

"You bastard," said Alison, coiling back a punch of her own, "we're through." And she nailed him with a straight cross that could have dropped a bull elephant.

The gun dropped out of his limp hand, Leo's eyes rolled back, and he crashed to the old red carpet with a thud.

Out!

The room erupted in applause, a cheer going around, people gathering near. Several of the younger working guys got in close, and one of them produced cuffs, pulling Leo's hands behind him. Even as they pulled him to his feet, he was still having trouble holding consciousness.

I looked at the two women. "Geez. Remind me never to piss the two of you off!" I said.

Alison was sort of bouncing, jumping up and down in one spot from excitement, clutching her fist at the same time. "Ow, ow, ow, ow! Leo, you bastard, ow! We are SO through."

Marty said from behind the bar, "I'll get you some ice for that, hon."

My father was standing beside me and clapped a hand on my shoulder. "Just remember this incident with regards to all women and it will stand you in good stead when you finally get married," he said.

Nora snorted. "Liam Quinn, married? Never happen. He's got these blind spots about women …"

I gave myself a self-pitying sigh. "This is the part of the story where the hero gets picked on by everybody who cares about him, right?"

Nora leaned over and gave me a kiss on the forehead then whispered, "Don't worry Liam. You know when we mock you, we mock you with love. And besides, Alison's sort of the hero here, let her bask."

My brother Davy leaned over my other shoulder and said quietly, "Yeah… nice job, sport. You let a woman win the big fight for you."

Ain't that just like family, to be so appreciative and supportive?

Yeah. And ain't that just like Philly? City of Brotherly Love. Millions of people, some getting along, some not. And I did my part; I'm not going to run up the Museum steps and raise my arms or nothing, because …well, it's been done.

45.

Inside the joint, things move on prison time. That means it all hangs on scheduled things like lunch, exercise break, dinner and lights out. It also means that anything that needs to get done gets done slowly. It's just the nature of skirting the law constantly, being careful.

Benjamin "Benny Toes" Valiparisi had gained weight. Given that he was not exactly svelte when we were serving time together, that was saying something. He looked like he'd swallowed an opera singer.

"Quinn, my old friend," he said through the meeting room glass. "You... You!" He pointed at me with a knowing index finger. "You said you'd visit and here you are. I mean... it took eighteen months, but who's counting when you're doing a few hundred years consecutive?"

"How're you keeping Ben? They treating you good?"

He nodded. "You know it. Nobody messes with a member of the Terrasini family in here. You figure otherwise? Don't start worrying about me, Quinn. I figured by the time you got out of here, you'd have grown a pair. You start blubbering, you'll go and make me think otherwise."

I chuckled at that, which was the reaction he wanted. "Listen, I need you to do me a solid," I said.

He smiled and cracked his knuckles together. "You know there's no words I like more on this planet than 'I owe you one, Benny. So, what is it? You need me to bust someone's head open or something?" He didn't even worry about the guard by the door or the camera. Benny Toes carried weight, with the kind of allegiances that could make life difficult.

"I need you to reach out to your friends at Schuylkill

pen. I've got an old friend there who's hiding some money. I need that money recovered and returned to the authorities."

He took a deep breath through his nose and squinted slightly, looking past me. "You can't even say it, can you? You want me to get some square joe to cough up his winnings so you can give it to the cops."

"Well.... I can SAY it, Benny. But I didn't expect putting it that way was going to win me any favors..."

He tsk'd me. "Quinn, Quinn, Quinn.... I love you like a brother. But you forget, I don't give a damn about nobody but me and the family. So as long as you're willing to owe me one.... I'm willing to lean on just about anyone you like."

"Better yet," I suggested. "Have him call the number I leave with you and turn the money in himself. That would make everyone's day, pretty much."

He studied me one more time, rapacious, a predator deciding whether I was worth chewing into. "You realize what this means, right, Liam?" He didn't typically call me by my first name. It should've meant a sign of endearment but instead, it sent a shiver down my spine.

"Yeah. Yeah, I get it comes with a debt attached."

He shrugged. "Then it's done. Consider it as such, anyway." Benny Toes got up and hung up the phone. He finger-pointed a gun at me and then mock pulled the trigger, before blowing smoke off the end of his finger. Then he turned his back to me and headed towards the grey steel door, and life inside Curran-Fromhold.

Nora was waiting for me in the parking lot, behind the wheel of her little Miata. The weather was sweet, and she had the top down. Still, I probably looked ridiculous in that little thing, half my torso sticking up out of it. I slammed the passenger door as I took the seat beside her.

"You didn't have to do this," she said. "My father... his pride would be wounded if they had to pay out the painting.

But you solved a pair of homicides and a major theft. If he didn't get the client's work back, that's not on you."

"I realize that."

"So what did you have to promise your old hoodlum friends." She said it with a tinge of bitterness. Nora didn't like me anywhere near that life. "Do I have to start worrying you'll end up back inside again?"

"Nah, nothing like that. It was nothing really," I lied. Whatever else it was, owing Benny Toes a favor was most certainly not "nothing." But the less she had to worry about my idiot self, the better.

"And did you find out whatever it was that you needed?"

"Soon enough. Only, Pat Delaney's call's going to someone else."

She raised her eyebrows at that. She knew how much money was on the line if I recovered the Vermeer. Life changing money. 'Repay the courts in full' money.

"Someone else? Who, exactly?"

When we got to the family home, everyone was out other than Davy, who was off shift.

He was sitting alone in the dining room, shirtsleeves rolled up, a cold Michelob on the table ahead of him."

"Liam, Nora."

He tipped the bottle our way.

"Mind if we join you?" Nora asked. Before he could answer she began to wander toward the adjoining kitchen door. "Liam, you want a beer?"

"Sure."

Davy got up and wandered over to the window, looking out into the night. "I hear they recovered that painting, and the money from Pat's heist. Quite a coup, that."

"Thank you," I said. "I don't screw up everything,

believe it or not."

He looked back our way. "Uh huh. Funny thing, though... they went and gave the credit on it to Bill Trevanian. I guess Leo insisted on calling him up in person and telling him where the painting could be found, and Pat did the same. That means you don't get your big payday. That would've been ... what, a quarter million, at two-point-five percent of twelve million?" Davy whistled. "That would've squared you right out of the gate with the courts. You'll probably never get another shot to do that, to clear it all away."

"Probably not, no."

"You'll be picking away at that debt for years."

"Yeah..."

"You'll probably never have a dime to rub together..."

I think I sighed a little, audibly. "Are you trying to cheer me up, or...?"

"Huh." He stared at me warily. "What is it with you? What the Hell am I supposed to think about you, Liam?"

"Could today's verbal assault maybe verge in the direction of something specific? Could you do that for me? I'm tired, David."

I hadn't called him 'David' in a long time, not since he was little and I was tasked with babysitting him. "Sorry," I added. "That was short."

"What I meant was, which guy are you? Are you the cynical crook with the flash BMW and the prison gangster friends? Or are you the brother I grew up with, the one who's more likely to get his head beat in sticking up for someone else than taking something for himself?"

He had plenty of reasons to feel that way; probably always would. "Davy..."

"Did you make a call to one of your jailhouse friends? Because I heard Leo Tesser is so scared, his hair turned white;

and Pat is talking like a tour guide on a summer afternoon. Which is good, because Bill is a good man and a good detective. But... it's bad for you. You not only don't get your money, you also maybe owe some goombah a favor."

"Maybe."

"Is that so? Because I know you think it was the right thing to do..."

"It WAS the right thing to do."

"Yeah..." He paused. "Sorry. 'Right' is the wrong word. 'Smart.' I know you think it was the smart thing to do."

I shrugged. "If you'd asked me six months ago to take that deal..."

"It's not six months ago, Liam. You're not inside anymore. You don't always have to end up with the short end, just because you done wrong in the past." He looked down at his shoes. "And I'm glad for that."

Then Davy walked over to the front door, pushed it open with his shoulder, and headed out into the cool Fishtown night air.

"Ma said she'd be back from Bingo by eight. Goodnight, big brother," he said, before letting it swing closed behind me.

I'm not sweating the quarter million. No siree, Bob. Nope. Not even thinking about it. Not. One...

Okay, it's going to sting for a while, I'll admit.

And I'd be lying if I didn't say a cool quarter-million wouldn't have felt like some sort of redemption, at least for the ten seconds it resided in my bank account.

But there will be more work, other cases. There have to be, or I'll never pay off those damn fines.

My phone rang. I checked the screen but didn't recognize the number. I let it kick over to my voice mail and put it back into my pocket.

It rang again.

Seriously? Fine. Just… fine.

I answered. "Quinn."

"Huh. You the guy?"

"The… Which guy?'

"Are you the sonuvabitch who hit me in the face with my friend's pool cue?"

Okay, that wasn't how it happened, but… "Let me guess: Abel Larsson? That you, pal?"

"You know damn well it is, you lousy Irish bastard…"

I looked at my imaginary watch.

"Pal? Did you just wake up or something, sweetness? That was a week ago."

Nearby, Nora slumped down in a dining room chair and rolled her eyes. "Good grief."

The biker was spinning out, mad with beef. "I've been inside. Just made bail. Guess what: I'm coming looking for you."

"Now, Abel: if you do that, I'm just going to have to knock you on your fat duff again. And this time, I'm going to have to drag you to the nearest precinct myself, so that I'm eligible for any reward stemming from the inevitable ensuing charge and conviction. I mean… breach of bail conditions for one, I imagine…"

"I'm going to beat you so badly, Army plastic surgeons will use you as their 'before' photo," Abel suggested.

See, it's the small details that make guys like Abel interesting, the times when they really put in an effort. It's the little things about this job I love. The psychotic bikers and mobsters of the world.

Me? I'm just trying to pay my dues, make things better again; make things right in the City of Brotherly Love.

Oh… hey, and maybe get back some brotherly love of my own, right? Maybe if I can do that, I can make my folks proud again.

It's a good place to start.

THE END

Liam Quinn returns in the second of the series, "Quinn Gets His Kicks,"
available now!

Want to stay in touch?

Get information on new releases by joining my mailing list at ianloome.com! Cheers!

Ian

ABOUT THE AUTHOR

IAN LOOME is the author of the hit LIAM QUINN MYSTERIES, the JOE BRENNAN spy thrillers, and the soon-to-be-released ROGUE WARRIOR thrillers.

Loome, who originally wrote as LH THOMSON and SAM POWERS is a veteran former news reporter and lives with his partner in Canada.

You can contact him online at https://www.ianloome.com

Made in United States
Troutdale, OR
08/04/2023

11809008R00139